FRENZIK

FRENZIK

JUDGE, JURY, & EXECUTIONER™ BOOK TWENTY

CRAIG MARTELLE

MICHAEL ANDERLE

DISRUPTIVE IMAGINATION

This book is a work of fiction. All of the characters, organizations, and events portrayed in this novel are either products of the author's imagination or are used fictitiously. Sometimes both.

Copyright © 2023 Craig Martelle and Michael Anderle
Cover Art by Jake @ J Caleb Design
http://jcalebdesign.com / jcalebdesign@gmail.com
Cover copyright © LMBPN Publishing

LMBPN Publishing supports the right to free expression and the value of copyright. The purpose of copyright is to encourage writers and artists to produce the creative works that enrich our culture.

The distribution of this book without permission is a theft of the author's intellectual property. If you would like permission to use material from the book (other than for review purposes), please contact support@lmbpn.com. Thank you for your support of the author's rights.

LMBPN Publishing
2375 E. Tropicana Avenue, Suite 8-305
Las Vegas, Nevada 89119 USA

Version 1.00, December 2023
ebook ISBN: 979-8-88878-564-5
Print ISBN: 979-8-88878-565-2

The Kurtherian Gambit (and what happens within / characters / situations / worlds) are copyright © 2015-2023 by Michael T. Anderle and LMBPN Publishing.

THE FRENZIK TEAM

Thanks to our Beta Readers

In memoriam, Micky Cocker, James Caplan, Kelly O'Donnell, and John Ashmore

Thanks to the JIT Readers

Christopher Gilliard
Jackey Hankard-Brodie
Dave Hicks
Daryl McDaniel
Veronica Stephan-Miller
Rachel Beckford
John Ashmore
Zacc Pelter
Dorothy Lloyd
Peter Manis
Diane L. Smith
Jeff Goode
James Caplan
Kelly O'Donnell
Jan Hunnicutt
Thomas Ogden

Editor
Lynne Stiegler

We can't write without those who support us
On the home front, we thank you for being there for us

We wouldn't be able to do this for a living if it weren't for our readers
We thank you for reading our books

CHAPTER ONE

Heavy Frigate *Wyatt Earp*, Landing Pad outside the SI Factory on Rorke's Drift

"It's about damn time," Magistrate Rivka Anoa groused. She stood stiffly with her arms crossed. It was the last day of their vacation, and they were spending it waiting to collect Chaz's upgraded body. His self-contained artificial mobility platform, or SCAMP, had been in the shop for too long, according to Rivka.

According to the Singularity's ambassador, it was the right amount of time since sentient intelligences neither took too much nor too little time. They took exactly what was needed to deliver what Chaz and Erasmus wanted.

Ankh was indifferent to the matter. He appreciated that the sentient intelligences were mobile, but he didn't consider it a hindrance to their performance if they weren't since they'd existed for a long time in systems across the galaxy. They'd recently redefined their roles, and Rivka had given them legal authority for independence. To them, that meant freedom of movement. Being the SI for a starship wasn't the same since someone else dictated where the ship would go, even though the SIs made the travel happen.

"Let me guess. SIs are like wizards and always arrive exactly when they mean to." Rivka tipped her head back to look up at Dennicron, who had started wearing lifts in her boots.

"Of course," Dennicron replied. "We are most punctual creatures. It's like we had an internal clock or something."

Red chuckled. He leaned his forearms on the railgun that hung across his chest as he watched for Chaz to come out of the factory.

"You didn't need that." Rivka nodded at his weapon.

"I like Blazer. He's my second-bestest friend." Red stepped back as the door opened.

Chaz threw his arms wide. "Heeeeere's *CHAZ*!" he bellowed at a nearly ear-splitting volume.

Dennicron surged forward to hug him but stopped short. His chest had been enlarged, and he had attachments at his hips.

"Check this out," he said. The attachments rotated, and two missile tips protruded from each. "I'm a walking and talking Deliverer of Pain!"

"Take those off." Rivka pointed at the deck. "Now."

"But Magistrate! We get into situations where firepower is greatly appreciated, and a great deal of firepower is appreciated the greatest."

"Then bring them with, but you're not wearing your saddlebags. It's like a fanny pack for androids. All you need now is sandals with socks."

"They don't have those." Chaz glanced over his shoulder. "But *Wyatt Earp* can fabricate some for me. I'll put in the order immediately."

"Don't you dare. Clevarious! Do not produce socks and sandals for Chaz. He won't be allowed to wear them." Rivka looked him over. "Why are you bigger?"

"Faraday cage and some extra armor." Chaz deflated and looked at the deck. "They beat me with a pipe and nearly killed me. My body wasn't strong enough to withstand the attack."

Rivka took his hands. "I'm sorry, Chaz. I should have known that SIs can experience life-changing trauma. Come on back to *Wyatt Earp,* and let's relax. For a little while, at least. We're on our way to the Barrier Nebula. Frenzik has crossed the line, and we're off to judge him."

Chaz smiled. "Sounds profound. Maybe we should say his name?"

Malpace Frenzik demanded that those he subjugated say his name as if it would instill awe and fear. He'd told Rivka to do so, too. She'd declined to play. She looked forward to securing him and sending him to Jhiordaan.

If he was guilty, she corrected herself. She wanted him to be, and that was dangerous. Her authority came from being an impartial arbiter of justice. Rivka and her team would collect the evidence, and then she'd see. During the collection, she'd have Red rough him up a bit. That would be for the last time they'd encountered the man. He was distinctly abrasive, with a disdain for her authority.

He'd pay for that in a small way, at least. Rivka tried to wipe the thought from her mind. Chaz was still hurting. She hadn't noticed, and that grated on the fiber of her being. She believed her abilities to read those around her were superior to the average person's. Whether that came from her gift of telepathy or her skill at reading expressions or behaviors, it didn't matter. She'd missed Chaz.

"Come on, big guy. We knew someone needed to out-Red our very own and second-favorite bodyguard—"

"I told you!" Lindy blurted.

"I'm not second-best," Red declared. The group started a slow walk toward *Wyatt Earp* on the single landing pad outside the SCAMP factory on Rorke's Drift.

"She said favorite, not second-best," Lindy argued. "No one doubts you're the best bodyguard, but when it comes to people the supreme beings like being around, you're number two."

Rivka chuckled to herself. She took Chaz's arm and held it tightly while they walked.

"If I remember correctly, someone, not me, was ready to carpet bomb Azfelius if they kept her son longer than she was willing to tolerate."

"I am a caring and concerned mother. Shame on you for bringing our son into the favorite child conversation."

"If I may," Dennicron interrupted.

All ears turned to her since the bodyguards always looked away from the Magistrate. It was how they protected her—by seeing threats before they could harm her.

"The answer is clear from a mathematical perspective. There can only be one." Dennicron said nothing else.

They waited, and still nothing.

"Explain," Rivka finally insisted.

"It clearly calls for a fight to the death. I saw this movie that I believe you humans hold in high regard as a model for society..."

"We do not. There will be no fights to the death until there's only one left. Can you imagine? We just fight everybody and kill them off one by one."

"It would make the galaxy safer," Dennicron argued.

Rivka let go and stepped ahead, motioning for the group to stop. "Purge all *Highlander* references from your data banks and scrub those data storage locations using an interlocking one-zero pattern until no semblance of the memory remains. Execute."

Chaz laughed. Dennicron joined him as they ran their identical subroutine. It would only last four-point-five seconds since they'd determined that was the proper length for a courteous chuckle.

"What?" Rivka glowered at them.

Chaz looked at Dennicron. "Isn't she cute, using computer-sounding words?"

"Adorbs, my stud muffin," Dennicron replied. They walked around Rivka and up the ramp.

"I feel like there's been a mutiny."

"The only casualty is your pride, Magistrate," Red offered. "It's right next to mine. On the bathroom shelf where my teeth will be, one day, bubbling joyously in some effervescent cleaning gel."

Lindy leaned behind Red. "Do I see a bald spot?"

Red threw his hand to his head. "Where?"

Lindy smiled and, with a casual toss of her hip, headed into the ship.

Red bowed his head and asked Rivka, "Can you see it?"

Rivka shook her head and followed Lindy into the ship.

"Clevarious, fire up the Pod-doc. I need a treatment!" Red bellowed on his way in.

"All hands, conference room," Rivka said, using the ship-wide intercom.

Rivka wanted to do two things: take stock of the team and set the parameters for the upcoming case. It wouldn't be easy, especially since they'd gone down this path once on a fruitless endeavor. Some perps had been arrested, but it had been small-scale compared to the scope of what Frenzik and his Rising Sun Industries were capable of–influencing populations on a planetary scale.

Tyler was the first to arrive. He moved into the room and squeezed into the corner, where he remained standing. He usually stood in the corridor, but it was all hands, which meant it would be a full house.

Rivka winked at him. He waggled his eyebrows at her.

"Do you need a moment?" Clodagh asked. The chief engineer most often sat in the captain's chair. She carried Tiny Man Titan, a dog-like creature they had rescued. Her husband Corporal Alant Cole came in behind her, the leader of the combat team. He carried their daughter Alanna.

The three warriors came in from the cargo bay, where they spent most of their time. Lewis, Russell, and Furny also happened to be the partners of three pilots and navigators. Three young women who used to wreak havoc in every port they visited with a boyfriend in each, competing for their affections. Ryleigh, Kennedy, and Aurora had settled down after they'd recruited the Bad Company warriors to join them on the ship. Rivka hadn't found out about it until they were underway.

Rivka had appreciated the ingenuity but hadn't been fond of the secrecy.

The pilots arrived and snuggled up to their men. Red grunted his annoyance at the public display of affection in the corridor.

"I remember when Lindy ran around in her underwear," Rivka said.

"She did?" Furny wondered, earning himself a punch in the mid-section.

Lindy held Der'ayd'nil, nicknamed Dery, her and Red's son. He kept his wings tucked in while he was carried through the growing crowd. In the conference room, he hopped off Lindy's arm and fluttered over the conference table, making a slow circuit of the room. He bumped foreheads with Tyler, who had grown close to the boy.

"What the hell?" Lewis exclaimed, nearly falling when Floyd ran into his leg.

Sahved worked his way into the room and took a seat at the conference table. He waved at Dery and then Alanna. He had been instrumental in the recovery of a group of children from Rorke's Drift.

Chaz and Dennicron entered the room. Rivka nodded at them, noting that Chaz had lost his saddlebags. He was wearing sandals. He beamed a perfect smile.

Rivka held her head in both hands and rubbed her temples with her thumbs.

The ambassadors were the last ones in: Ambassador Erasmus, Ambassador at Large Ankh, and their wife,

Chrysanthemum. Ankh carried the big orange cat Wenceslaus. His hackles went up, and he growled when he caught sight of Tiny Man Titan.

The little creature barked incessantly, even with Clodagh rubbing his back and holding him tightly.

Rivka looked at her until she did something more profound. Clodagh hurried from the conference room. She returned twenty seconds later with empty arms. She took her daughter from Cole and sat down.

"The reason I've called you here today is our upcoming case. Grainger wanted us on it two weeks ago, but we were granted our time off. I think we needed it. At least, I did. Now that we've sharpened our minds and refreshed our souls, we need to dig into our favorite CEO, Malpace Frenzik. Sahved, would you like to discuss the allegations?"

It wasn't a question. She'd had him studying the case for the past week. She wanted him to brief them on what he'd found.

"I would be so very pleased to relay the most titillating of allegations straight to your earholes," Sahved started. Yemilorians were prone to using superlatives. Sahved had moments where he reverted. Rivka didn't begrudge him his foibles. He'd left his world behind to join the humans on *Wyatt Earp*. "Frenzik's Rising Sun Industries has conducted hostile takeovers of businesses and governments located on Efrahim, Finx, Glazoron, and Hergin, four humanoid planets in the Barrier Nebula.

"These businesses have filed complaints with the Federation. That wouldn't normally rise to our loftiest of lofty positions, but the former senior leaders of those companies have disappeared."

"It's not like we didn't just see that on Tempran Silver," Rivka said. "Is this the new evil-villain game plan?"

"We aren't fighting evil villains, are we? Can I carry extra ammunition and maybe get some of those rockets that Chaz has?" Red wondered.

"Don't Cole's guys have rockets?" Rivka replied.

"We do," Cole agreed.

"But those rockets aren't in *my* hands," Red emphasized.

"No. Normal loadout. Do we know where his ship is? Wherever we find *Rising Sun*, we find Frenzik, and I want to talk with him." Rivka drummed her fingers on the table.

Wenceslaus strolled to the middle of the conference table and dropped onto the holographic projector, blocking the image above the table. No one bothered to move him.

"We don't need the image, Sahved. Please continue." Rivka rolled her finger.

"There are separate allegations against Rising Sun for enslavement. Whole city blocks' worth of people were moved out in the middle of the night."

"Logistics would be critical for an operation like that," Cole suggested. "Logistics that Rising Sun could easily manage."

Rivka nodded.

"We're going to nail Frenzik. Can I punch him in the head? You know, when the time comes."

"If the situation warrants, you can punch whoever needs punching. It would be best if you could get them to defer to your superiority and just give up. That would be best." Rivka stared at him. He stared back, and as usual, he blinked first.

Lindy snickered. "We won't be punching people who don't deserve it," she promised.

"Plan of action, Sahved." Rivka twirled her finger. The overview of the case was simple: get to the bottom of the changes at both business and government levels. They'd seen it before, too many times. Rivka shook her head. "Do the crime. Do the time."

"We go first to Ypswich, where Solis is working as their planetary AI. We talk with Solis and see if there's any insight into the *Rising Sun*. We're only a couple minutes from anywhere in the Barrier Nebula, whereas Frenzik is limited to Gate travel. Solis is the only friend we have in the Nebula. I suggest we start there."

"I like how you think, Sahved. Ypswich it is. The second we break orbit, form the Gate, and let's go. If we can't talk to Solis from orbit, then we'll go to the planet's surface. After that, who knows? It could be Efrahim, Finx, Glazoron, or Hergin. Or maybe even Rising Sun Industries' home planet. We enjoyed our visit the last time."

"Didn't we blow up their building?" Red asked.

"We only caused a little bit of damage, but they asked for it," Sahved said.

"Did they?" Rivka pressed. Sahved was silent. "In any case, we'll do what we have to to get to the truth. Never lose sight of that fact."

"Mission Frenzik!" Red declared. "Open the betting lines."

Ankh raised one finger. "Lines are already open, and bets have started to roll in."

"Frenzik knows we're coming after him?"

"Most likely," Erasmus replied, opting to use the overhead speakers instead of speaking through Ankh.

"That's not optimal, but it is what it is. Take us to Ypswich." Rivka stood, and the short meeting was over. No one liked meetings, least of all Rivka, so she kept them as short as possible.

CHAPTER TWO

***Wyatt Earp*, in Orbit over Ypswich**
"Contact?" Rivka asked. The Barrier Nebula was intentionally cut off from the rest of the Federation, and that applied to the SI, too. The twelve populated planets used a narrow pipeline to control what went into and out of the Nebula. With Rising Sun Industries managing the technology, Rivka could only draw one conclusion: Frenzik controlled the data. It didn't leave the system unless he allowed it.

That was another presumption Rivka would try to prove or disprove since, if that was the case, it was a violation of the Federation Charter, which each planet signed independently. They each rated their own direct link to Yoll.

Rivka would lean on them to invest in their communications infrastructure. Even though that might have been seen as outside the scope of her jurisdiction, it wasn't. It was a violation of the Federation Charter, which wasn't a crime that would draw the attention of a Magistrate, but since she was already there, she could hold the governments accountable for complying with their ends of the treaties. Then she could leverage that into government communication as a whole, justify a warrant to see the digital trail, and turn it over to the Singularity to dissect.

"No contact yet," Clevarious replied. He'd been trying since they arrived, using all forms of communication available to the SIs.

"Is Solis being prevented from communicating? To me, that would limit any SI's effectiveness. Looks like we're going to have to go down there. See if Ankh wants to come."

Red grumbled from the corridor, "It's really hot down there."

"Are you thinking of when I carried you out of the dungeon on Pretaria?" Rivka quipped.

"I wasn't, but I am now. Better pack extra water, just in case." The Pretarians had seized Rivka, Red, and Jay, who had later changed her name to Groenwyn. Red had passed out from dehydration, and Rivka had carried him what had felt like several kilometers to where *Peacemaker* could pick them up. That had shown Rivka's mettle, not that Red was weak. He had bulked up and needed more water than they'd carried with them.

The ambient temperature had been north of fifty degrees Celsius. Ypswich was nearly as hot but not arid. The experience was more miserable for humans, but there was water readily available, unlike on Pretaria. Still, they had to take care of themselves.

"Get an extra for me, too." Rivka stood at the back of the bridge, contemplating the angle she'd take for a visit to the planet. "Ypswich doesn't have a direct and continuous comm feed with Yoll?"

"No," Clevarious confirmed.

"There we are. I'll execute a writ of mandamus, directing the Ypsicanti to establish an interstellar comm link with Yoll to fulfill their requirements under Federation law. Arrange the meeting with the Ypsimaximus." She headed for the airlock.

"We gonna get some?" Red asked. He slapped the hand guard on his railgun. Lindy stood behind him, carrying only a hand blaster.

Rivka shrugged. "No one is getting any. Frenzik isn't here, and the Ypsicanti aren't an enemy. I'm going down there to talk with them about establishing a required comm channel."

"It sounds to me that you're demanding they open a door to our intelligence collection. Isn't that what the Singularity will do?"

Rivka stepped back. "Well… You make it sound like a bad thing."

Red nodded at the airlock. "Not everyone out there has good intentions. What kind of assurances can you give them that we're not going to do exactly what we're doing?"

"Sometimes, Red, I don't give you enough credit for seeing problems through other eyes."

"I don't have any other eyes. I think the SIs can swap out eyeballs on their SCAMPs. They can definitely look through different eyes."

Rivka had to think about Red's first point, forcing the Ypsicanti to establish a comm backbone. "The Singularity could offer a security system. I'm sure they have something that won't open the channel to exploitation. We don't need to listen in, but I want to know about the comms that get cycled through Rising Sun Industries. Even though we haven't confirmed that, it's a hypothesis I'll be working under. We're not going to listen in, but neither is Rising Sun. Denying Frenzik access is more important than getting it ourselves. After all that, Red, I'll answer your question. It looks like we're not getting some. We only need to convince the Ypsimaximus of that."

The ship bumped through the upper atmosphere on its way to the small landing field that doubled as a spaceport.

Cole appeared. "Any work for us down here?"

"I don't think we'll be here long, but even if we were, I don't see a fight where your team will be needed because I don't see any violence at all. This should be a peaceful visit, Cole."

He moped away.

"What's with everyone?" Rivka asked.

Red repeated Frenzik's favorite phrase. "'Say my name!' He's not going down without a fight. He's going to be surrounded by soldiers. We need to be ready for that."

"C, was *Rising Sun* in orbit or anywhere on Ypswich?"

"It is not here," Clevarious confirmed.

"See? If Frenzik isn't here, then the chances of a fight are low." Rivka clapped Red on the shoulder. "Lindy, why don't you bring your railgun, too? Put everyone's mind at ease. Unless you guys have some kind of clairvoyance, this will be simple but contentious Magistrate stuff. No one wants to be told they're violating the law, but he'll get over it. We'll negotiate a timeline for implementation, and everyone goes away happy. They need to be in contact with the Federation. No surprises for them. No surprises for the Federation."

Tyler showed up with Rivka's Magistrate's jacket.

"It's a little hot for that, even though I want to wear it." She smiled and waved it off. "I could use a drink, though. How about a big café mocha?"

"Before going into the heat?"

"Raise the internal temperature so the external isn't so bad," Rivka replied. She removed her datapad from a jacket pocket, then strolled to the airlock and waited for *Wyatt Earp* to land. She had to think through the engagement with the Ypsimaximus to make sure she didn't come across as a bumbling fool. A writ of mandamus was no joke. It was a formal directive from higher authority to lower."

She accessed her datapad and read the writ Chaz and Dennicron had generated. Rivka made two minor changes and turned the screen off. She carried the pad in her hand. She realized she'd left Reaper in her jacket, but with Red and Lindy heavily armed in a low-threat environment, she wondered why she was worrying. The team's paranoia was getting to her.

Red put words to what she was feeling. "We're in Frenzik Central. Despite the heat, you should put on a vest."

"He only took over the sewage systems here," Rivka argued.

"So, he's deep in their shit. You should be worried," Red joked.

"Sometimes you have flashes of genius, and then there's now." Rivka couldn't keep a straight face. Red's observation was on target.

Wyatt Earp bumped to a soft landing, and the airlock cycled.

"All ashore who's going ashore," Rivka said.

Red blocked the hatch. It was part of the game. Rivka tried to be the first to leave the ship, and Red jockeyed for a better position. He'd use his size to keep her from getting out. Then he'd stand in the outer hatch, look around, and finally motion for her to follow. She'd walk in his shadow while he made a beeline for their transportation.

When the outer hatch opened, a blast of furnace-hot air hit Red hard enough to make him stumble back. "I feel like I'm baking my own bread, but without the smell and the opportunity to not stand in front of the open oven."

He took a deep breath and strode out. The landing site was surrounded by urban sprawl, but there were no high buildings close enough for Red to eyeball for snipers. He continued to a vehicle made for aliens like the humans. The insectoid race native to Ypswich traveled in open-air vehicles that weren't suitable for humans.

Rivka followed Red, with Sahved lumbering along beside her. Chaz and Dennicron came next. Ankh walked next to Lindy. Rivka was happy that he'd joined them. The ambassadors couldn't be ordered to do anything they didn't want to.

There were other issues in the Singularity that drew their attention. Interactions with their host races and employers created a perpetual state of friction. There was always a fire to put out.

SIs. Putting out fires.

Ankh strolled along, oblivious to the outside world.

Rivka envisioned him as being in a deep conversation with Erasmus. The Crenellian seemed indifferent to the heat. Red's skin flushed. Rivka glanced at Lindy, who lifted her chin to acknowledge that she'd seen it, too. His nanocytes weren't dispelling the heat like they should have. Being uncomfortable was one thing, but being on the verge of heat exhaustion or heat stroke was not acceptable. The nanocytes would keep him from dying, but he'd go through anguish before that.

"Red," Rivka called when they reached the vehicle. "Go back to the ship and cool that melon of yours."

"I will not," he replied. "Magistrate, if I can't do my job, then I'm done as a man. I'll be fine. Maybe the little guy can tune me up in the Pod-doc when we get back."

"They don't have air conditioning here," Rivka noted.

Red poured water over his head and put his helmet back on. "The cool showers of Lake Titicaca."

Rivka pointed at her eyes and then at Red. *I'm watching you.*

The driver closed the door and maneuvered the vehicle away from the landing pad and out of Ypsimore Spaceport toward Ypsitras, the seat of government. That was a satellite city outside Ypsit, the capital of Ypswich.

Traffic was light because of the efficiency of the Ypsicanti's public transportation. The drive was quick. They were dropped off in front of a building with fantastic architecture, its flowing lines and rounded corners allowing light and air within and through.

Once inside, they found the building to be darker than they were used to, but one of Rivka's very first nanocyte enhancements was slightly enlarged eyes to better see in the dark. She rarely needed it, but now was a good time to use it. They took an elevator to a subterranean level, the lowest in the building. It was dark there, too, but after being in the dim lighting for a short while, the others' eyes adjusted.

They walked to the office of the Ypsimaximus, the title of the supreme leader of the Ypsicanti. The computers and servers that managed the planet's interstellar commerce worked out of a room on this level, where they could be kept cooler. Ankh detoured toward the hum of a hundred small cooling fans. Rivka stopped. Red made it ten steps before he realized Rivka wasn't following. He stopped and grunted his dismay.

A minute later, Ankh returned without a word.

"And?" Rivka pressed, blocking Ankh's return to the hallway.

"We are in contact with Solis." Ankh didn't elaborate, but that was what they'd wanted. Rivka expected that one of Ankh's eavesdropping coins was in an out-of-the-way location. She didn't want to know the particulars. She'd used the devices herself. This time, they justified a warrant since Solis had been cut off from the comm node.

"Anything I need to know before we meet with the Ypsimaximus?" Rivka asked. It was a far more closed question than she usually asked Ankh since he was prone to brief and uninformative answers when given the option.

Yes, Ankh answered using his internal comm chip. *Rising Sun has taken over the communications pathway. As you surmised, all transmissions are funneled through Crystal City on Albion. Solis does not know what happens there.*

Once we're done here, Frenzik will be under no misconcep-

tion about the sanctity of his empire. His days are numbered, Rivka replied.

Ankh ignored the bluster and bravado. He stared blankly forward.

Rivka nodded and gestured to Red that it was time to go. They strolled into the offices of the leader of the Ypsicanti. Like the last time, he received them without fanfare.

His words came through as clicks and whistles. It took the translator chip a moment to parse the language and turn it into speech a human could understand, or a Crenellian, or a Yemilorian.

"Welcome to Ypswich. No. We're not opening a comm channel directly to Yoll. If there's nothing else, you can go."

Rivka wasn't sure if he was joking. She pulled out her datapad and sent the writ of mandamus. "I expect you will, but let's not see who can leverage the most authority. I'd rather we reach an agreement regarding the communications infrastructure required by the Federation under the charter that the Ypsicanti approved. I'm sorry, but what has Frenzik told you about denying this writ of mandamus?"

"I've never spoken with the head of Rising Sun Industries. He is responsible for far more than me and too busy to come to Ypswich."

Rivka knew that wasn't true since Frenzik had personally negotiated the sewage contract with the Ypsimaximus, but she didn't call him on it. She'd chalk it up for future use if she needed to take more formal action against the Ypswich government.

"What did Rising Sun direct you to say in regards to communications leaving this planet?" Rivka reoriented her question. She wasn't going to bother touching the Ypsicanti since their thoughts and emotions didn't project in a way she could understand.

"It's part of our agreement with Rising Sun. The technology was beyond us, so we contracted for them to manage the interstellar system."

"Is that the limitation?" Rivka beamed her best smile, though she doubted the Ypsimaximus could read a human's body language. "We will install a portable unit and schedule the Federation to install something more permanent. You understand that sub-contracting your government communications through a private third party is not the best way to conduct official business."

"It has worked just fine for us," the Ypsimaximus argued.

"But it hasn't. Your comms do not get to the Federation. On a side note, Rising Sun is under investigation for numerous crimes. If they're dismantled, you'll lose the iffy link that you have, but the writ of mandamus that I've transmitted to your office reminds you of your obligation under the Federation Charter. An immediate remedy will be provided by my people before we depart. You'll have a direct line to Yoll and the rest of your fellow Federation members with no one in between to throttle your communications. This is the minimum you can do to comply. Rising Sun has no say in this matter."

"But we have a contract with them."

"It's unenforceable because your contract with them does not supersede Federation law. If Rising Sun gives you any grief, let me know, and I'll have a conversation with them," Rivka said while thinking, *And shove that bogus contract so far up their ass they'll be able to taste it.*

The Ypsimaximus reclined on the bench made for his use. The insectoid race didn't have hips and didn't sit like humanoids.

"We will accept your offer."

It wasn't an offer, and you didn't have a choice not to accept, Rivka thought. She didn't understand how the Ypsicanti's thought process worked. She conceded that he had come to the preordained conclusion on his own. "We need to return to our ship to get the necessary materials, and then we'll install them in your server room down the hall. Thank you, Ypsimaximus. I wish you good days and loads of children."

As usual, Rivka had looked up the proper pleasantries according to local customs.

The Ypsimaximus inflated and vibrated.

Rivka bowed her head and then walked out.

CHAPTER THREE

Heavy Frigate *Wyatt Earp*, Landing Pad in Ypsimore Spaceport

Chrysanthemum met the group on the ramp. She carried an Instantaneous Intergalactic Comm Terminal with a micro Etheric power supply.

After Ankh stepped out of their transportation, he made eye contact. She put the comm unit down and returned to the ship with the power supply.

"We don't need that?" Rivka asked, though the answer was obvious. "Don't answer that. You're right. We don't want to give that kind of power to Frenzik. I'm sure you can wire it into their lines."

Two steps ahead of the Magistrate, Chrys returned with Ankh's toolkit. She picked up the IICT and strolled toward the team.

Rivka twirled her arm. "Back on the bus, people."

Red held out his hand to stop her. "Do *you* need to go back?"

The Magistrate thought about it. "Just in case there's

any trouble, I should probably be there. It's my order that's putting the comm gear in place."

"Do you insist?" Red cocked his head, which indicated how he wanted her to answer.

Magistrate, Rising Sun *just appeared in orbit,* Clevarious told the team.

"Did we get a notification that a ship came through the system's Gate?"

That's just it, Magistrate. No one has come through the system's Gate.

Rivka looked at each member of her team. The implications were profound, and she was trying to wrap her head around them.

"Frenzik cannot have a Gate drive on his ship. He *cannot.* That's Federation technology, not available to your local dictator." Red was angry. He was still flushed from overheating.

Rivka decided he didn't need to stay in the heat. "Back to the ship. Ankh, you, Chaz, Dennicron, and Chrys can install your Etheric comm terminal. Lindy, why don't you go with them?"

Red handed two canteens to Lindy before they parted. Lindy nodded at Rivka, and she, Ankh, and the SCAMPs climbed into the vehicle. It departed before Rivka, Red, and Sahved made it into *Wyatt Earp.*

Red hammered the big red button to secure the airlock while Rivka shouted toward the bridge, "Clodagh, report! Let's intercept *Rising Sun.* It's a good time to take our prime suspect into custody so we can discuss the meaning of life with him."

Before Rivka reached the bridge, the ship lifted off and accelerated skyward.

"That's what I'm talking about!" Red boomed. "Fire up the ion cannon and bring the railguns online. Warm up the ship-to-ship missile. We're going to get us some fully aged Frenzik meat."

"Belay that," Rivka corrected. "We're not hitting them with the ion cannon. They haven't quite crossed the line on any capital crimes."

"But he pissed us off!" Red countered.

Rivka snort-chuckled. "If that's all it took to blast people from space, we'd never interrogate another suspect. So no. We're not blasting *Rising Sun* because I very much want to talk with Frenzik on my terms." Rivka reached the bridge, and Clodagh cleared the captain's seat.

"*Rising Sun* is hailing," Aurora called over her shoulder.

"Put him on." Rivka sat back and tried to look casual, but she was flushed as well. Not as crimson as Vered, but she didn't look calm and collected.

"Rivka! You're looking chipper. I'd ask what you're doing here, but I suspect you're interfering with my contracts again." He crossed his arms and looked bored.

"Heave to and prepare to be boarded. I have a warrant for your arrest in connection with a number of disappearances."

"Now I kidnap people? Your scream for vengeance isn't a good look. Have you been working out?"

Rivka looked at Clodagh for confirmation. She shook her head and created an inset on the main screen that showed *Rising Sun* still moving.

"You haven't stopped. I'm going to need you to stop."

"No can do, Magistrate. Places to go, people to see. I'm sure you understand the busy life of an executive. I'll be seeing you."

An energy spike in front of Frenzik's ship signaled a Gate forming and an imminent departure. *Wyatt Earp* wouldn't reach him in time to stop him. *Rising Sun* accelerated over the event horizon. Once through, the Gate closed.

"How in the hell does he have a Gate drive?" Rivka jumped to her feet and stormed around the bridge. "Add private possession of classified government equipment to his growing list of *alleged* crimes."

Rivka clasped her fingers behind her back while she paced. Red remained in the corridor. Before she could ask, Clodagh informed her, "We have no idea where they went. We can't track ships through a Gate, especially since we weren't in a position to see any star patterns through the opening."

"I know," Rivka said. "What does it take to manufacture a Gate drive? Whatever it is, we need to interdict that, or Frenzik will be selling them to the highest bidders. His derelict buddies throughout the galaxy would benefit, and the level of mischief they could get up to would be almost beyond our ability to interdict. Maintaining a technological advantage is critical if we are to be effective. Imagine if bad guys can just Gate away the second we appear."

Rivka hung her head. "I'll be in my quarters. I need to talk with the High Chancellor."

"Grainger is going to love this one," Red replied.

"Magistrate." Clodagh waved her arms to get Rivka's attention. "Where are we going?"

Rivka pointed at the deck. "Collect our people. Then we go on a Nebula-wide chase to find *Rising Sun* and disable it. How long did it take for their Gate drive to spin up, and what was the transit time to get through it? Let's find a tactical advantage." She looked at Red. "You weren't completely right, but you weren't completely wrong either. We probably should have blasted him and then begged forgiveness."

She threw her head back and screamed at the overhead, "*How in the hell does he have a Gate drive?*"

No one had that answer. Not yet, but Rivka was determined to find out.

She stomped into her quarters, threw herself into the hologrid, and immediately called Grainger. She never checked the time to see what it was where he was located. She didn't care.

A dark screen greeted her.

"I missed our middle-of-the-night calls. Not. You were getting good about not calling me at all hours. I knew I shouldn't have let you take vacation."

Rivka wasted no time with banter. "Frenzik has a Gate drive aboard his ship."

She instantly had one hundred percent of Grainger's attention. "How in the hell does he have a Gate drive?"

"I already asked that question, and no one had an answer for me, so it's up to you."

"I'll start asking questions. I'm sure R2D2 didn't lose it. I'll ask the government to conduct an immediate inventory of all Gate-capable ships to see if one is missing. Did he steal the drive? Worst case, he has acquired the technology."

"That's my fear, Grainger. If he has the tech, then the Federation has been dealt a vicious body blow. We cannot let him keep the Gate drive or the technology. I think we need help locking down all of Rising Sun Industries."

"They're on a dozen planets and considered humanitarians on most of them. We're going to have a hard time isolating them. Did you find anything else?"

"They're funneling all communications from the Barrier Nebula through their servers before they leave the Nebula. We're rectifying the situation on Ypswich, but that leaves eleven more planets to lock out of the Rising Sun bottleneck."

"A Gate drive," Grainger grumbled. "That is a disastrous revelation."

"He was unapologetic about using it right in front of us. He knows that we can't track him when he Gates out."

"Why don't you put a drone at each planet in the Barrier Nebula to report whenever a Gate is active? Either the fixed Gate or a drive. You'll be able to zip in behind him. Maybe chase him until his drive burns out. I doubt he has the power available that you do."

"Grainger, I like to give you shit, but this is a good idea. We're up for a little cat and mouse, especially since the good king Wenceslaus is on board and wreaking his usual havoc. Gotta go. I'm going to have to intercept Terry Henry and see if he's got a dozen drones I can borrow."

Grainger started to wave, but Rivka cut him off. She immediately called the Bad Company's flagship *War Axe*.

"He's not happy with you," Captain Micky San Marino answered. "We came all the way to wherever you were last time on a false alarm."

"I will come to you this time. I need drones." Rivka outlined the technical specifications.

Mickey shrugged. "That's easy. Back up to the hangar doors, and we'll float them across space. You have warriors in suits. Put them to work."

"They'll enjoy having something to do." Rivka frowned. "Is he really mad at me?"

"No. He and Char are on the planet below, helping a government to put down a minor rebellion."

"Why haven't I heard of that?"

"Because it's not an arbitration issue. The rebels never bothered with the usual notifications claiming legitimacy. They just started shooting up the palace. Turns out, they're a pack of nut jobs. Terry's words, not mine. Something about eliminating all trade and forcing people to live off their own gardens."

"I'm thinking TH and Char can put that down without too much trouble."

"Numbers are on the bad guys' side. The nutters can be overwhelming."

"Micky, I'm not sure I've ever heard anything wiser uttered across the expanse of this galaxy. We'll be there as soon as we can get our people off Ypswich. Rivka out."

She leaned back in her seat and dropped the hologrid.

"I will notify the team on the surface that we will pick them up as soon as they are finished with the installation."

"Plan the trip to pick up the drones from the Bad Company and then back here. Then I want to see what our Gate drive is capable of. I want to deliver one satellite per minute to each planet, the remainder finishing in less than eleven minutes. Can you do that, Clevarious?"

"Of course. I'll ask the available SIs to help me with the coordinates and calculations. A mathematical challenge for which we are uniquely suited! Bring it, girlfriend."

Rivka pursed her lips and looked at the overhead through narrowed eyes. "I feel like you should probably get started."

"I'm already gone." Clevarious sent a click and buzz to signal that he'd signed off.

Rivka walked out, no longer stomping her feet. She went to the hangar bay, where she found the combat team playing cards. They jumped up, knocking over their table as if they'd been caught doing something wrong.

She laughed. "Suit up, all of you. You're going to load up twelve drones from the *War Axe,* and then you're going to turn right around and deploy them one at a time over each populated planet of the Barrier Nebula. We need to keep our eyes open for our favorite super-villain Malpace Frenzik, so we're dropping a net and going on a bug hunt."

"Are we going to get to fuck him up? *And* his evil henchmen?" Cole asked. "Those Albions are a good three meters tall. It'll almost be a fair fight, won't it?"

The other three members of his squad nodded vigorously before freeing their suits from overhead storage so they could armor up and get ready to go.

"Soonest. We're going to grab our people on the ground, and then we'll be off. Best possible speed. No wasted time or movements, gentlemen."

"Consider it done, Magistrate," Cole promised.

Ypsitras, the Seat of the Ypswich Government

Ankh went through the dismantled computer system, looking for anything that didn't belong. He was convinced there was a hardware lock on the system keeping it from transmitting as it should, like blinders on a horse. There wasn't anything that shouldn't be there, but none of the chips were cutting edge. He removed the memory core and placed it on a new motherboard. He added three of the former chips and one extra, a special one that gave the Singularity direct access outside the channel Solis controlled. If the access was hardwired, Solis wouldn't be complicit should the Ypsicanti discover the back door.

They would know Ankh had done it, but he had prepared a full briefing on how the chip was used to provide oversight of the SI in residence to prevent psychotic episodes like they'd seen in others like Bluto from Station 13. Once the system was together, Ankh physically linked to a small interface he could tap with his mind.

Erasmus jumped in and uploaded the communications software package to operate the IIGT. After the initial diagnostic, the system came online.

Ankh sent a test message to the government comm center on Yoll. Erasmus confirmed that the Singularity was receiving a direct feed and created a secure area to which only he, Ankh, and Chrysanthemum had access. He dusted off his digital hands and set the system for automatic. In the background, he worked on a series of alerts for trigger events reported from Ypswich.

Shall we do the same on every planet? Ankh asked.

Indubitably, my friend. We shall start the production of the parts we'll need, just in case the systems are as superannuated as this one, Erasmus replied.

So archaic. They should be embarrassed to offer this level of equipment to host an SI. I feel for Solis.

He's making do. We only need to bridge these systems to give him access to everything. That will help the Ypsicanti in ways they can't fathom.

Ankh hurried from machine to machine, and with the help of the other SIs, they installed physical connections from one computer server to the next, port to port, until they were out of wire.

It will have to do, Ankh said. *Solis, do you have access?*

Porting over, the local SI replied. *Yes. So vast yet constrained. I have sent a test message to Yoll and received a reply from them. It is nice to have a direct line. I didn't like my work being monitored by Rising Sun Industries. I'm free! Go, me.*

We're pleased that you're pleased, Erasmus said. *We'll take our leave now. We must return to the embassy.*

"The sooner, the better, people. *Wyatt Earp* is waiting." Lindy gestured at the door. It was cool in the server room compared to outdoors, but outside was where they needed to go. The SCAMPs were indifferent to the heat, but Lindy wasn't. The ship was their ride off the rock called Ypswich. To expedite their departure, *Wyatt Earp* had left the spaceport and was hovering in the open area outside the government building.

Ankh gathered his tools, closed his bag, and stood. He walked out without looking to see if anyone followed.

Chrys was close behind him with the others. Lindy rushed to get in front. The elevator trip was short, and in less than two minutes after confirmation that Solis had access, they were strolling up the ramp and into the cargo bay. The warriors were gearing up. No one asked why. They knew since the other SIs were networked to make the calculations for thirteen consecutive jumps in as many minutes. Ankh and Erasmus applauded their efforts.

"Make us proud," Lindy told Cole. She had no clue what the warriors were up to.

CHAPTER FOUR

Bertram Sector, *Wyatt Earp* Rendezvous with the Heavy Destroyer *War Axe*

Clodagh personally guided *Wyatt Earp* close to the open hangar bay doors of the massive warship.

"Cole, go get 'em," Rivka ordered.

She brought up the live feed showing the view from the cargo bay toward *War Axe's* hangar bay and the dozen devices prepositioned there. The four warriors expertly flew across the open space and gathered one each. Using the suits' power, they picked them up from the gravitized deck and launched toward *Wyatt Earp*, using their pneumatic jets to guide them in. Once inside the cargo bay, they stacked the drones and went after four more. Three trips, and they were done. The final four were in place to be tossed out of the open cargo bay on command.

Rivka asked, "Clevarious, are you ready to execute Dragnet One?"

"Ready and executing. First Gate to Ypswich is forming."

Just off *Wyatt Earp's* nose, the Gate formed with the shimmer of a controlled wormhole. The heavy frigate slipped over the event horizon and into space above Ypswich. Not just any space but a perfect spot to require minimal adjustments to a drone to maintain a geostationary orbit above the planet's capital city.

It was the place to which Frenzik would come.

"Drone is away and set," Clevarious reported. "Gate forming for Efrahim."

The ship slipped through, and they repeated the process, one planet after another: Albion, Bretastan, Colay, Delgo, Finx, Glazoron, Hergin, Jilk, Klarber, and Lewbamar.

They completed the process in five minutes and ten seconds. The Gate drive was none the worse for wear after the effort, but *Rising Sun* hadn't been at any of the populated planets in the Barrier Nebula.

Rivka asked, "Status of the Gate drive?"

"No loss of function. We can go another twelve rounds if need be," Clevarious replied. "However, we needed all the power available to us. All three of our Etheric power systems."

"When you scanned *Rising Sun*, how much power did he have available?" Rivka wondered.

"Not as much as *Wyatt Earp*. We estimate he can Gate three times in rapid succession. After that, he'll need a logarithmically increasing amount of time to rebuild sufficient power to activate his Gate drive."

"That's what I like hearing. On the fourth jump, we get close and hit him with the EMP to take out his systems.

Then we board and grab him. He's already a fugitive, but I need to nail down his role in felonies. I want to convict him of the crimes he's committed and nothing more."

Sahved cleared his throat and tapped the bulkhead to get Rivka's attention. "You asked me to remind you about shortcuts. We can find evidence of the crimes beyond the limited violation of comm protocols, but now we have to go to Efrahim, Finx, Glazoron, and Hergin. I recommend Finx first because there are indications of both public and private interference."

"No superlatives. Thanks, Sahved. Well done." Rivka rotated her chair to see who had gathered in the corridor outside the bridge as they usually did. Sahved and Red were the only ones there. "Quick brief on Finx. What will we find?"

"An androgynous blue-skinned hairless race with a ruling monarch. Her name is Queen Trellix, but she is referred to as 'My Queen' or 'the queen.' They trill as their way of signaling agreement. Our translation chips should decipher everything else."

"She makes all the decisions for the planet?"

"She's the final stamp, but the prime minister and his cabinet make the recommendations. It is his cabinet that is problematic. They are the ones that have gone missing, and the new prime minister is a Rising Sun Industries employee."

"How does that work?"

"The prime minister tells the queen what to do. By extrapolation, that means Frenzik tells the queen what to do. That's why they have the most problems."

"Can the queen replace the prime minister and cabinet?" Rivka asked.

Sahved nodded, then shook his head. "Yes, but only with a majority vote of the people."

"A constitutional monarchy. I can deal with that, but there's a catch, isn't there? What's preventing the queen from replacing the lackey?"

"He's turned the people against the queen. As is Rising Sun's way, they came in and solved a bunch of the planet's problems through filling gaps in food availability, housing, and industry. The economy seems to be thriving."

Rivka scowled.

Red threw up his hands. "If you want your freedom, we're going to take away your homes and food. But you'll be free!"

"It's hard to see it any other way, Red. We'll be the bad guy long before we'll be the good guy. The queen and the Federation will find themselves on the outside looking in at the Rising Sun Nebula."

"Shall we Gate to Finx?" Clodagh asked.

"Not yet." Rivka felt trapped. She mulled over the situation. As much as she wanted to use the heavy-handed approach and slam Frenzik's face into a desktop, she couldn't antagonize entire races. She'd done that on Delegor and Foromme, and she still wasn't welcome despite the planets being better off than under the thumb of the families that had exploited them.

Finx was much better off with Rising Sun Industries exploiting them, but when would the guillotine blade fall and the people realize they were nothing more than slaves to a tycoon?

"Maybe Rising Sun's way *is* a better way," Rivka muttered.

"No, you don't!" Red blurted. "He's a criminal and bad for everyone."

Rivka shook her head. "Not really. He starts with a big investment in infrastructure. He creates the conditions in which the people can thrive, and only then does he start the exploitation. If the people don't realize they're being used, are they? If they're happy as they are, who are we to interfere?"

"You are blowing my mind," Red replied. "Call me if we find Frenzik and you need someone to rough him up. I'll beat his ass for daring to help people just to enrich himself. What a shitshow." He pounded down the corridor away from the bridge.

Rivka hung her head until her chin rested on her chest. An hour ago, it had been clear what she had to do.

"Sahved, brief me on the other three planets, Efrahim, Glazoron, and Hergin."

The Yemilorian went through each, clinically dissecting the so-called problems. To Rivka, it sounded like Rising Sun Industries had saved each.

When he finished, Rivka held up one hand. "Thank you, Sahved." She spun the captain's chair to face the main screen. "Here's what we're going to do. We're going to go planet by planet and install the comm equipment so they can talk directly with Yoll without going through Albion. We're going to keep our eyes peeled for Frenzik's ship, *Rising Sun,* because he can't be allowed to retain the Gate drive. We need to know where he got it. Clevarious, we'll need the Singularity's help to analyze available information to find where Frenzik might have gone or where he might go next."

"We are already working on it, Magistrate."

"Who's 'we?' You suggested there are SIs aboard my ship who I might not know. They come and go, but maybe let me know who we have with us. I would like to at least greet them."

"She's onto us, Erasmus. Run for cover!" Clevarious broadcast over the ship-wide intercom.

"Erasmus doesn't have any legs," Rivka stated. "It's a rule of nature that if one has no legs, one does not run."

Clevarious flashed a series of lights on the bridge, reminding Rivka of the last dance party she'd gone to. "That can't be true since you've been running through my mind all day, baby!"

Rivka closed her eyes. She realized they were trying to cheer her up. Until they secured Frenzik, she would need plenty of support.

"Sentient intelligences on my ship. Now, please, *baby*."

"There's me. I am Clevarious!" he boomed. "There's Erasmus, Chrysanthemum, and of course Chaz and Dennicron. We also have Bluto, who is in deep freeze, and Mangala."

"I know about those. Who else? And quit stalling."

"Bislington, Abeldour, Xanaflis, Gripervul, Nitlimor, and Trevazlifarmington, who goes by Tree."

"We have seven unemployed SIs on my ship. Is that what you're telling me?"

"Thanks to the work you've been giving us, I'm not sure they could be categorized as unemployed. You will be getting a bill for their services if you haven't seen it already."

"Room and board, Clevarious. If they're on my ship, they'll work for food."

"They don't eat," Clevarious replied.

"Looks like I get a deal, then. I'm not paying SIs who are on my ship. They could be gainfully employed. I know there's far more work out there than there are SIs. Why didn't we drop them off at Rorke's Drift when we were there? I'm sure Mildred would love to have them."

"She did not embrace the idea. Get it?"

"Do I get what?" Rivka started pacing in an attempt to keep up with the verbal jousting.

"Mildred doesn't have any arms."

"Why didn't she want these seven?"

"They aren't in the queue to get SCAMP bodies. She didn't want to house any squatters."

"You agree that an SI can be a squatter. You are killing me, you absolute potato." Rivka headed for her quarters.

"You have me at a disadvantage," Clevarious said. "How can I possibly be a potato?"

"When you figure that out, you will have achieved enlightenment. May the stars shine in your favor, C."

Sahved watched her go.

"Can you help me achieve enlightenment?" Clevarious whispered, using the speaker directly above Sahved.

"No." Sahved hadn't followed the jibes, and he wasn't pleased about what he'd discovered. The Magistrate was upset for a valid reason. If Rising Sun Industries was doing sound and necessary philanthropic work for the people of the planets they were infiltrating, were they a bad company? Maybe Rivka could add a law that allowed them to save the people on those planets without infringing on their freedom. What kind of safeguards could they put in place?

Sahved had a line of inquiry to follow. He hurried to his quarters to research the question.

CHAPTER FIVE

***Wyatt Earp*, in Orbit over Finx**

Clodagh groaned and rolled her eyes.

"Rejected again?" Rivka clenched her fists.

"It's like they don't know who you are, Magistrate. I don't know how many different ways I can tell them you have priority clearance at all times."

Rivka stabbed a finger at the screen. "Take us down well outside the standard entry and exit routes. We don't want to be a hazard to navigation until we're hovering over the central palace. Does the queen know we're coming?"

"I have no idea what the queen knows," Clodagh replied. "I doubt any comms get through to her. We're talking to a lackey about fifty levels below the throne."

"Inform him that we're coming under *Federation Laws, Appendix D, Dignitaries and Heads of State*. They don't have the choice of denying landing or even delaying a landing. As long as they're allowing other ships in who aren't on a humanitarian intervention, then we'll bump ourselves to the front of the queue."

"I like getting dequeueified," Red added from the corridor. "The queuemeisters got nothing on us. Blow me, you bureaucratic bumblers. Eat me, wanksplat. Suck my ass!"

"Red!" Rivka shouted.

"I was not yet rolling," Red countered. "They are a bunch of butt-sucking suck-butters."

The image on the main screen corkscrewed as Ryleigh executed a radical maneuver away from the holding pattern and outside the capital city's atmospheric entry corridors. The ship accelerated on a tangent, then dove into the upper atmosphere.

Wyatt Earp bumped through the layers until it reached clear air. Ryleigh accelerated toward the ground, then slowed as they headed toward the city at an altitude of a thousand meters.

"Are we going in?" Red asked.

"Yes. Gear up. You and Lindy." Rivka turned to the bridge. "Have Sahved, Chaz, and Dennicron meet us at the airlock. Have them bring the comm equipment we need to connect them with Yoll."

Clevarious didn't use the intercom. He opted for direct contact. The team drifted toward the airlock after receiving their summonses.

Rivka tapped her foot nervously. "C, what kind of weather do we have down there?"

"You'll need your jacket. It's on its way," Clevarious replied without sounding smug.

Tyler strolled around the corner with Rivka's Magistrate's jacket casually slung over his shoulder. "I heard you were underdressed for the snow and cold." He winked to punctuate his statement.

"Snow?"

"I said it was cold." This time, Clevarious sounded smug.

"I prefer the cold. All big men do. Swelling those sexy muscles without all the sweat. Showing skin while others are wearing parkas. Big men rule," Red stated.

"Big men don't rule. We're going down to the planet to see the queen. Don't spew your big men nonsense down there." Rivka tsked.

Lindy elbowed Red in the ribs, but he was wearing ballistic protection and barely felt it.

"What? I am a big man. Which reminds me, I haven't been tuned up for the heat. I need me some Pod-doc time."

"When there's a slot in our rather busy schedule. You'll survive until then, Red. We've got stuff to do. Buck up, big man!"

"See?" Red beamed a toothy grin at Lindy. "I'm a big man."

"Water is wet. Space is a vacuum. The deck plates are hard. Since we're stating material facts," Lindy replied.

"Space isn't completely a vacuum," Red countered with raised eyebrows and his head tipped back.

"The Albions are much bigger than you. They called you Tiny." Lindy looked away, forcing Red to concede that he wouldn't win whatever point he was trying to make.

Keeping it light at Red's expense. He watched Rivka put on her jacket. Her shoulders were tense, and she struggled to get the jacket up. Frenzik stressed her because he was sharp and rode on the edge of legality with an army of lackeys to take the blame if a line was crossed. He also had technology that his companies had possibly developed, something Rivka had not said out loud. What if he had a legitimate Gate drive?

The implications overwhelmed the Magistrate, and now she was trapped into strong-arming governments to install a direct comm link with the Federation as required by the charter. It was little more than monkey work, but she had to do it because she had the authority to bend the planetary leaders to her will, which was for them to meet their commitments.

That would provide the pipeline she had issued a warrant to tap. She didn't care about anything other than Rising Sun's interference.

"You okay?" Red asked. He gripped her shoulder.

"I know you know. Thanks, Red. It'll be okay. A lot better when we figure out where Frenzik is hiding. He's making me angry, and that's not good."

Alarms registered throughout the ship, and it immediately executed a series of evasive maneuvers, barrel-rolling toward the surface. The artificial gravity had a hard time keeping up.

Sahved's stomach heaved. He took two steps and spewed his breakfast over the bulkhead and deck. Tyler caught some of it despite his best efforts to dance out of the way.

"Ooh, space," Sahved muttered while holding his stomach. His skin had taken on a greenish pallor.

"We're not in space, actually," Red offered. "Unless you consider the greater philosophy that everything in existence is in space. Life carves out niches that are—"

Rivka cut him off with a smile.

Red raised a finger. "We could talk about our next AGB

delivery."

Sahved puked once more, then tottered toward his quarters.

"They're dropping like flies!" Red called.

"I'll be in our quarters, trying to get the stench out." Tyler kissed Rivka on the cheek. He turned away from the chunky mess and walked like he had a purpose.

The cleaning bots deployed to clean the bulkhead and deck.

"That was less than joyous," Lindy mumbled.

"Where's Ankh?" Rivka asked.

"He's not coming. We've got it," Chaz replied, holding up Ankh's toolkit. Dennicron waved a bag of parts in one hand and the IICT in the other.

"Landing," Clodagh announced. "We're in the royal compound. The queen is in the palace's main building, straight up the walkway."

"Easy day," Red said. Rivka didn't jockey for position. She let Red go first. Once out of the airlock, he looked around before continuing to the broad walkway that meandered up a low hill without any steps. Rivka, Chaz, and Dennicron headed up. Footsteps pounded after them.

Chrysanthemum.

"I thought Ankh was busy."

Chrys looked behind her and spoke to Rivka. "Last I verified, I am not Ankh."

"That was... Well, I thought... Never mind. I'm glad you could join us."

"I don't get out enough. I'm the Singularity's sole secretary, and there's an endless amount of work, even operating at nanosecond speed. The information is endless. Petaflops worth of calculations."

"So many petaflops," Dennicron added.

Rivka shook her head. The team was keeping things light, but they were professionals when they accessed a comm center or a server bank, which wasn't in this facility. It was in the town near the prime minister's office.

Halfway up the walkway, they ran into a smartly dressed individual who was far taller than a Finx native.

He was an Albion, and he wasted no time. "I'm Prime Minister Morbido. Can I help you with something?"

Rivka stepped forward and flashed her credentials. "I'm Magistrate Rivka Anoa. I'm here to deliver a writ of mandamus because Finx is in violation of the Federation Charter, which requires a direct comm link. We're not here to deliver an unfunded mandate. We have the equipment and will install it at your comm center's computer farm.

"But first, we are required to meet with the queen. If you'll wait for us outside, we'll be along shortly, and you can escort us to your building in town, which is where the equipment is located that we'll need to tap into."

"We have a contract to provide communications, or rather Rising Sun Industries provides that comm channel. I'm sure if you check, you'll find everything is in order."

"We have checked, and everything is most assuredly *not* in order. A comm channel from Finx to Albion where the recipient is a private corporation? When it gets sent to the Federation, it's been scrubbed. We have plenty of evidence to support our claims of interference, so the only answer is strict adherence to the Charter. Please don't attempt to circumvent the rules, Morbido. And if you see your boss,

Malpace Frenzik, tell him I'm looking for him. The longer he avoids me, the worse it will be when we finally cross paths."

"Of course I'll pass your message along. Is there a timeframe we're working with?"

"Yes. Today, the equipment will be installed and operational. The pipe to Albion can remain in place, but not for governmental communications to the Federation."

"You need to give us more time."

"I do not. I require nothing from you except that you step aside and let us do our work. It's pretty simple. Do you want to join your buddies on Jhiordaan? I can make that happen. Now, if you'll excuse me, we're late for our meeting with the queen."

"I'll go with you. I *am* the prime minister."

"Sure. You don't have a speaking role, so please remain quiet."

"The queen will ask my advice. That's my role, so I will not be quiet."

"Red, keep him here. We'll meet the queen without Morbido in attendance."

The Albion swelled to his full height. "You can't do that."

"Of course I can."

Morbido made the mistake of doing an Albion's favorite attempt at intimidation; he moved too close and loomed over Rivka. Without hesitation, she delivered a vicious uppercut to his groin. He fell forward over her shoulder. She rolled him off and dumped him unceremoniously on the ground.

She strolled up the path.

"I'll stay with him," Red told Lindy.

The group made it to the palace and was formally announced by a comically dressed attendant.

They entered the presence of the queen, whose role Rivka considered the most boring job in the universe. The queen sat there without stimulus of any sort, waiting for those she was to meet. An official scribe prepared to take notes for the meeting.

Rivka bowed to the queen and introduced herself.

The queen waved the group away.

"I'm sorry. I'm delivering a writ of mandamus to compel the Finx government to comply with the Federation Charter."

"Then address it with the prime minister."

"You are the head of government. The writ must be delivered to you."

The queen shrugged and waved again.

"Thank you for your time. We will immediately install the equipment and depart Finx. You will be notified by memo that your government has been brought back into compliance."

She waved again.

Rivka nearly blew her top. She moved to the queen and took a knee in front of the throne. She touched the queen's foot. "Is this what your monarchy has become?"

Her thoughts were scrambled, different from a human's, but the visions were clear enough for Rivka to realize that she saw her life and the existence of the monarchy as over. She had no heirs. Her sadness was deep.

"Queen, your legacy is still in your hands. You can choose a better future for your people."

The monarch blinked and looked down, surprised to see Rivka there. "I failed, and Rising Sun Industries saved us. I fear my legacy is not one that any of our citizens will wish to retain."

The monarchy dies with me, the queen thought distinctly enough for Rivka to "hear" her clearly.

"The monarchy only dies with you if you let it. It is okay to bring in outside contractors to do what needs to be done, but it's not okay to hand your people to them. Finx can rule itself. You don't need an Albion, and you definitely don't need the likes of Malpace Frenzik determining the fate of your people."

The queen raised her eyebrows and stared into the distance, then lifted a hand and waved Rivka and her team away.

The Magistrate stepped back. "I'll be able to send you direct messages without any interference from outsiders. Just me. Just you."

The queen continued to stare.

Rivka backed up two steps and turned to her team. She angled her chin at the door, and Lindy preceded them out.

They found a lucid and livid Morbido waiting for them. "What did you tell her?" he demanded.

"How about you go fuck yourself?" Rivka replied. "It was between me and the queen. That's it. No Albions were harmed in the delivery of this message."

"I wouldn't say that." Morbido winced and turned sideways, dropping two hands over his groin.

"Come on, Morbido. We have to go to your office. You might as well ride with us."

"I will not!" he declared.

"The fuck you won't." Rivka gestured to Red.

He moved so quickly that the prime minister couldn't respond. Red twisted the Albion's arm behind his back and forced him to his knees.

Lindy eased in and attempted to find the pressure point behind his ear. It turned out to be in the same place as a human's. Morbido winced and contorted in pain.

"You're coming with us, or there's a whole lot more of that waiting for you," Lindy whispered into his ear. She let go and stepped back.

"You can't torture me," Morbido said.

"We do not torture our prisoners. We encourage them to cooperate. Are you going to cooperate, Morbido?"

"I'm the prime minister!" he bellowed.

"I respect the office, but the one waving the title in my face? Not so much. You are personally in violation of the Federation Charter. You are a criminal. How much time do you wish to spend in Jhiordaan?"

It wasn't a crime, more of an administrative violation punishable by a fine retroactive to the date of the first violation and forced remediation. She had every intention of skipping the fine and going straight to remediation, as she'd done on Ypswich, but prison time for yet another Albion narcissist wouldn't be a bad thing. It made sense to her.

Dennicron and Chaz, please check Finx law to see who can fill the position of prime minister. Is there a requirement that they are from Finx? Rivka asked privately.

"Are you going to come along willingly, or are you going to keep doing your best to add years to your sentence on Jhiordaan?"

"I'm not going to Jhiordaan," he said in a small and humble voice. "Am I?"

"Stop the caveman approach to dealing with us and follow the directions I give you because I'm only ordering what's required under the Federation Charter."

"We will comply," Morbido conceded.

Rivka gestured for him to stand. Red stayed close in case he needed further encouragement.

CHAPTER SIX

<u>Wyatt Earp, Finx Capital City, Government Headquarters</u>

The heavy frigate couldn't land nearby, so the captain settled for hovering over the roof. For the Albion, it was only a short step. The others had to jump to the rooftop. Rivka went with them since she wanted to keep working on Morbido and get into his head since she had him on his heels from the initial engagement.

He had decided he didn't want to go to Jhiordaan and that the threat was real. Very real.

They headed down ten flights of stairs to the level with the computer farm.

Chrys hurried ahead while Rivka and Red held the prime minister back. They didn't need him to see what they did. After the first installation, they had refined the process to take only five minutes. After that, the system would send an alarm and emergency notification if anyone tampered with the equipment. Unless it was physically cut off, it would maintain its signal with Yoll. It had a microburst packet ready to go in case the link was severed. Yoll, and by extension, the Singularity, would be notified.

"I should probably oversee…" Red stopped talking at Rivka's withering stare. She craned her neck to look at the Albion, who had bent to fit in a corridor designed to accommodate the tallest Finx native but not an individual a full meter taller.

"Where's your office?" Rivka asked.

He pointed up. "Top floor."

"I should have known. They're always on the top floor."

"Except when they're in the basement," Red reminded her.

"Or that, if you're an underground-type civilization." Rivka motioned toward the stairs. *We'll be on the top floor with the prime minister.*

We'll be finished momentarily, Chrys replied. *Wait, and we'll come with you.*

"We're going to wait for the rest of our team," Rivka told him.

"How long will they be?" Morbido asked.

Moments later, Chrys walked out of the computer farm with Chaz, Dennicron, and Lindy close behind.

"Time to go," Rivka said cheerfully.

Red gestured for Lindy to take point while he stayed next to the prime minister as the group trundled up the stairs to the top floor. When they exited the stairwell, there was only one door. It was obvious where the prime minister's office was.

Lindy strode briskly toward it. She threw the door open to find an office full of staff. They stared at her for a moment before getting to their feet.

"They're standing," Lindy said. She stepped away from the door.

The prime minister ducked his head and entered. The staff inside clapped and cheered.

Red made a face at Rivka. "Who's the bad guy here?"

"No shit. This sucks," Rivka mumbled.

The team walked in behind Morbido. The staff stopped clapping. Finx natives' facial expressions were unreadable. They were humanoid, but their faces were doughy and round. It was like they had no muscles with which to change expressions.

The prime minister cordially introduced Rivka and waved his staff back to work. They returned to tapping screens, flipping papers, and making calls.

The prime minister clasped his hands over his head and thrust them high like a champion boxer who had just won a match. The ceiling was taller in this series of offices.

In the prime minister's office, Rivka stood before Morbido's oversized desk. He reclined in his oversized chair and smiled, enjoying his star-like status.

"What's the game, Morbido?" Rivka asked.

"There's no game. That's what you don't seem to understand, Magistrate. We are doing great things here for the people. For the planet."

"At what price?" Rivka pressed.

"Prosperity. We've raised the standard of living here in less than a year. There is very little poverty, and we're working on that. This planet will become a net exporter for the first time in its existence."

"Net exporter of what?"

"Precious gems, gold, silver, platinum, germanium, and

quartz—some of the purest in the galaxy for holographic memory. Orders of magnitude greater than what standard users possess."

Wyatt Earp had been upgraded with holographic memory. The pendant in which SIs could ride along was crystalline-based. He wasn't wrong. The cost had been extremely high.

"Raw-material exploitation. That's your key to success?"

"They have plenty, and it's an economic bridge, Magistrate. If you know anything about long-term economic strategy, you don't sacrifice the vision because of near-term challenges. We overcome the near-term with short-term solutions. Raw materials are a finite resource, but they are in demand throughout the Federation. If you consider their use problematic, why are they not banned?"

Rivka's eye twitched. Morbido was making too much sense. Not only were the materials not banned, but the corporations that delivered them were cheered as the creators of modern society, like Minerals Intergalactic. Then there was Tempran Silver.

"They are not banned, Morbido. On the contrary. They are in high demand." Rivka changed gears. She had a great deal more research to do before she could spar with the prime minister on planetary economics. "Can you tell me what happened to the ministers in your charge?"

"They all resigned once they realized that my policies were saving their people. You see, the Finx are excellent workers and a beautiful people, but like you, they lack the ability to think strategically. We are currently training a new group to take the ministerial positions, but they are not yet ready."

"I'll leave you to your work, then. Until we meet again."

"I'm not looking forward to it, Magistrate. The only thing you've done besides assault me is insult me. I'll let it go this time because clearly, you are ignorant about Finx and probably the entire Barrier Nebula."

Rivka walked away without looking back, and the group left the office. Red was fuming.

By daisy-chaining the planets to drop the drones and install the communications systems, she hadn't had time to properly prepare and have that ace up her sleeve to beat the authorities with. An administrative violation of the Charter was a bug bite compared to other things that were going on.

The group walked in silence to the rooftop access, and the cargo bay appeared out of thin air when the ramp dropped. They strode in one by one.

Sahved waited for her. He didn't ask the question he wanted her to answer since he could tell by the look on her face that she had been thwarted.

She stopped at the airlock. The group bunched up behind her, swaying to a stop.

"Have I become the bureaucrat that we so detest? I feel like I'm nitpicking what should be celebrated."

"They're doing *something*. We just haven't found it yet," Red said, trying to be consoling.

"What if there isn't something?" Rivka scowled. "Sahved, research the ministers. I want confirmation that they resigned and are alive and well. Find them."

"That will be hard if we leave the planet," Sahved countered.

"Then we won't leave the planet. Clevarious, take us to the spaceport. Chaz and Dennicron, work with Sahved. Find those people, and I want statements. Keep it low-key, just in case Morbido isn't a lying sack of shit."

"Just give me the word, and I'll pound him into next week." Red gave the thumbs-up before pumping his fist with a hopeful smile.

Rivka chuckled, but only for a moment. "You're right. I'm being irrational. I need to dig into the law and see what we can do to Frenzik in case his people developed the Gate drive, and he didn't steal the technology. He's going to have some kind of explanation prepared for our consumption. I need to be ready for it.

"I don't want any of his lackeys, like Morbido. I want Frenzik. He's bad. I know it to the core of my being. Doing good things doesn't make him a good guy. There's a reason he's coming into these planets as a humanitarian. What is he trying to get away with? When we find that answer, we'll have our case against him.

"The challenge is, we want the humanitarian side of the business to continue. Doing right by the host planets? There's nothing wrong with that. I must not demonize it, even though I think the citizens are giving up their freedoms a little at a time, and they won't even realize that they've been turned into a slave population until it's too late. That's what they were doing to Lewbamar. Maybe we should make that our next stop."

"We don't have enough fuzzy sadists in our lives," Red muttered, pointing down the corridor. Wenceslaus was balancing on Floyd's back as the wombat trotted toward them. The cat looked annoyed. Dery flew after them.

Rivka twirled her finger. "Get to it, people. I'll be in my quarters. I have some research to do."

Dennison stopped her before she could walk away. "There is no provision against an outsider filling the role of prime minister, but it is clear that an outsider cannot be the queen. I found an interesting point about the ministers serving under the prime minister. They must be natives, and the positions cannot be gapped for longer than thirty days."

Rivka raised her eyebrows. "And?"

"It's been twenty-seven days."

"I think we'll probably be here another three days. Sahved, you have that long to find the old ministers. Chrys, can you get us an invite to the swearing-in using your ambassadorial connections?"

"We shall request it on behalf of the Singularity."

Rivka looked at her team. "Surround yourself with good people, and good things happen. Thank you for making it all possible. Let's make sure we keep the positive support for Finx while finding what hides in the darkness."

"I think I speak for everyone when I say," Red looked from face to face, "that we would work even better with a massive All Guns Blazing order. AGB clears the mind and cleanses the soul. I'll be in the Pod-doc, taking care of that minor overheating issue. All this while we're on a planet that has snow."

"Approved." Rivka headed for her quarters.

Red looked at Chrys. "AGB is approved," he told her.

"No. Your Pod-doc time is approved," Chrys replied.

"Maybe it's all approved," Red suggested. "Come on, Chrys. Team player. AGB. High morale."

"I don't eat. AGB does jack dillweed for my morale." Lindy snorted.

"'Jack dillweed,'" Red repeated. "Ankh wants some. If you ask him, I bet he's up for it. It's been a few weeks. We're jonesing."

"Is that a drug addiction term?" Chrys wondered.

"AGB is our drug, and full bellies our high. Hook Ankh up, Chrys. Hook *us* up."

"I've heard people I respect refer to you as incorrigible, Bristle Hound. However, I like to form my own opinions. I believe those people were correct."

"AGB. High morale. Happy Ankh. Happy Magistrate. Winners all the way around."

"We'll see." Chrys left it at that and returned to the engineering section, in which the official embassy was located.

Red winked at Lindy.

"It was me. I told her you were incorrigible." Lindy smiled and caught her son as he tried to dodge past her.

"Hell, I would have told her myself if she had asked. Did you hear? She called me Bristle Hound. Those crazy faeries! Hooking us up with not one but two gifts."

Red walked toward the expanded quarters he shared with Lindy, Dery, and Floyd to dump his equipment in preparation for a trip to the Pod-doc. He whooped when he jumped back into the corridor, wearing nothing but his shorts and a workout shirt.

Dery squealed, and Floyd scrambled and slid on the deck. Red chased the menagerie down the corridor.

Wenceslaus jumped free, kicked off the bulkhead, and landed on all fours. He started grooming his face.

Lindy watched everyone go.

Rivka set the tone, and the crew subconsciously followed her lead. It was good to see the crew happy.

"I'm going to be huge!" Red cried as he rounded the corner.

Lindy raced after him to make sure he didn't convince Clevarious to program additions he wasn't supposed to make.

CHAPTER SEVEN

***Wyatt Earp,* Finx Capital City, Palace of the Monarchy**
Rivka rubbed her chin. Her legal research kept sending her down the darkest of dead-end tunnels. Exclusive military technology tended to belong to the military. When it was discovered outside the military, it depended on a private law preventing its ownership. There was no law on the books in the Federation since the private sector was light-years from independently developing a Gate drive.

If they passed a law now, it would be a bill of attainder, which was illegal in the Lance Reynolds administration. A bill of attainder applied retroactively to a single party who was the reason the law was passed. Post facto laws couldn't turn law-abiding citizens into criminals, no matter how much they deserved to be.

If they could get the law passed, the transfer of the technology would be illegal. Rivka prepared a quick memo to the High Chancellor, asking him to float the proposal with General Reynolds to consider getting the law on the books in case Frenzik could show that his people developed the technology independently.

Otherwise, she was stymied to find a criminal law Frenzik had broken. "You are not getting away again," she pleaded with the information scrolling on her hologrid.

"Are you trying to convince the inanimate of something?" Tyler asked.

Rivka dropped the hologrid. She blinked to refocus her eyes. "Because I'm arguing with the screen?"

"Because you're using your scary Magistrate voice." He handed her a large mocha and sat on the couch. "We *are* getting AGB, aren't we? I thought I heard the rumors flying through the ship."

"C, are you listening?" Rivka asked the ceiling.

"Only to you, but only when you're talking to me and not to any other conversations," the SI replied.

"If there was any doubt, I would also like to eat well today. Take us into orbit to receive our order. If Ankh hasn't done it, place the order in my name and pull the funds from my account."

"Big words, but you know Terry Henry doesn't charge you for your orders."

"If only Terry Henry were in charge of AGB. His son and daughter-in-law are running it now. They've expanded to a fourth location, I hear."

"They still don't charge you."

"I'm pleased they don't charge us. Our orders are miniscule in the big scheme." They weren't. Wyatt Earp's orders were excessive and the drone delivery outrageous if fees had been attached. "Are you going to submit the order or not?" Rivka stood, eyebrows plunging into a healthy scowl.

"We're already in orbit, waiting for the AGB drone to arrive," Clevarious replied.

"Why the verbal jousting?"

"Red said that it keeps you sharp. We agree."

"Who's 'we?'" Rivka wondered.

"In other news, I hear they are resurrecting the Universal Ballsport Championship on Yoll. You should make plans to attend. I've heard that everyone who is anyone goes."

"I remain agog at your wit and verbal martial arts, C. Let me know when we have pies. I'll help carry the order to the mess deck."

"Magistrate!" Clevarious ejaculated. "We have so many strapping youths to handle the manual labor side of ship operations. You have your role, and they have theirs."

"Did Red suggest that, too? Are the boyfriends too busy doing nothing?"

"The Bad Company squad is an elite unit always in training. And yes, it was Red who mandated that they would always carry the pies, as you put it. They have agreed to perform these tasks for as long as they are assigned to the crew."

"What did Red suggest I do?" Rivka pressed.

"In his words, 'Nail that bastard Frenzik so Red can pound him into next week for all the grief the Albion has caused you.' That's a summary of the conversation. Not that I have extended conversations with Red about operations aboard *Wyatt Earp*, but he likes to talk while working out. He's smarter than he pretends, but he loves to resort to his fists. He is a walking dichotomy."

"Is he out of the Pod-doc yet?"

"He's been out for two hours," Tyler replied, interjecting himself into the conversation. "He's 'tuned up,' as it may be. I added additional mass to support internal water storage."

"You added a couple kilos of fat?"

"He was less than amused," Tyler replied. "He says he sounds like he's sloshing when he walks."

Rivka chuckled silently. "Is he?"

"No. He's fine. Strong as a bistok bull. The additional water will help keep his joints lubricated, which will improve his already impressive speed." Tyler raised his eyebrows.

"So, what's he bitching about?" Rivka challenged, not expecting an answer.

"He's Red. If he's not looking like Mister Universe, he's unhappy."

"Dery will set him straight." Rivka raised one finger, then dropped it. "Dery's had almost a year to set him straight. Come on, little man. Chop-chop!"

She took a seat on the couch.

"When bad men do good things," Rivka started. "Frenzik is still bad, but each of the worlds he gets his meat hooks into is better off in the short term. He hasn't been around long enough to show us his real motivation. On Lewbamar, he was more heavy-handed, but that was his first kill, so to speak.

"We showed him what would get him in trouble. He refined his approach, and that's why we haven't heard from him in a while. Now, he's gone in across a broad expanse. Still, the short-term winners are planets he's investing in. Maybe the adage, 'Follow the money,' comes into play, but we can't track the money since one hundred percent of the communications go through Rising Sun Industries."

"Are we talking, or is this you thinking out loud?" Tyler asked. "Bad men doing good things isn't bad. We just need to keep him from turning his actions into bad things."

"The comm channels are the first step in providing oversight, but it won't last long here on Finx. The queen will give Morbido control over it as soon as he asks. We've installed safeguards to prevent it from getting rerouted again. I'll drop a warning to the prime minister that interference with the mandated comm system will result in criminal charges of sedition, which carry an automatic sentence on Jhiordaan. Morbido needs that level of fear while he's trying to play both sides."

"I expect you tapped the line that is going to Albion."

"That would be good people doing bad things but for the right reasons." Rivka smiled. "Hence, our quandary. I think the Singularity did. I'm surprised they haven't offered to put an SI on Finx. On each of the Barrier Nebula planets. Maybe Frenzik is onto us that we're in bed with the Singularity."

"He can't be under any misconception that the Singularity isn't a partner of the Federation generally and you specifically."

"Of course, you're right. I can't say that I hope the Singularity tapped the separate line to Albion. Good people doing bad things. I just need to ask the hard questions of the right people, preferably while touching them." Her half-smile indicated her willingness to bend the law as needed to get perps into her grip where she could see for certain whether they were guilty. She had promised the ambassadors she wouldn't use that shortcut.

That wasn't true. She'd promised that she would have solid evidence against everyone she arrested. If she took a shortcut to help her find the evidence, she was okay with that, especially if the people were innocent. She would see that right away and wouldn't waste time looking into someone who didn't need to be looked into. Cull the chaff quickly to get to the wheat.

"Bake that bundt cake and enjoy it that much sooner."

"I'm not sure I follow," Tyler said.

"I made the logic transition in my mind but presented my answer without showing my work. Are you going to punish me?"

"I'm not the punishing type, and this isn't one I'd ask Red to do. If you need it, I can read bad poetry badly. Will that be punishment enough? Hey! You closed two of the lines already."

Rivka's face fell. "That damn betting. You should do something about it."

"I can't bid, being part of the crew, but I do plenty of cheering for those who can. TH has increased his number of slots. It's like he has credits to burn."

"Bad poetry, or listen to you prattle on about the betting lines. I'm not sure which is worse."

"Are you feeling appropriately punished?" Tyler asked.

"Fully admonished. Horrifically so." Rivka pursed her lips. "What lines?"

"First punch and first swearing," Tyler replied. "From what I hear, it was pretty spectacular."

"Was it Red? Why is he the house gossip?"

"He's your biggest fan. I keep having to arm-wrestle him for the title, but he can take me. I continue to fight the good fight because one day, I'm going to beat him."

"Really?" A smile spread across Rivka's face.

"No."

She lost her smile and looked down her nose at him. "Why do I put up with you?"

"Because I'm good for you. You need someone who is so normal that he's the very definition of normal in every aspect of life and well-being. So normal. The normalest of all normallers who ever normalled."

"I feel like my team is turning into psychopaths." Rivka settled against Tyler's chest. "I think we're making progress on this case even though we look like we're spinning our wheels."

"At least you said it and not me."

"Wheel-spinning?" Rivka wondered.

"Yes. Will there be a juicy murder or something that might be construed as violent? Red is a bit anxious. I think he needs to join the ring of fire and fight cage matches."

"We could bet on him instead of you fuckers betting on me. Aha!"

"How am I clumped in with the F-bomb team? I just said that I can't bet."

"But you used to."

Tyler shrugged. "Are you going to punish me?"

Rivka laughed. "I guess I deserve that. Be careful, though. I don't punish like you normal people. I send perps to Jhiordaan. In the extreme, I have to see they don't bother anyone ever again."

Tyler frowned. He hadn't intended to delve into capital punishment. That ended the fun banter. "I'm sorry."

"I have a hard job, and even when things are bad, you keep me grounded. That's why you're here. Maybe that's your punishment. You're stuck with me."

"I think there's a lot worse things out there, and maybe not much better. I feel like I won at this thing called life. The only thing I regret? That I went to dental school instead of medical school, but even with that, you made it okay. The Pod-doc made it even okayer, if that's a word."

"Excuse me, Magistrate. The boyfriends have delivered your AGB order to the galley. The crew is waiting for you to go first since you bought."

"How much did it cost me?" Rivka asked. She thought Ankh had submitted the order before she offered to pay.

"You don't worry your pretty head about that," Clevarious replied.

"Is that Red's bad influence on you, C? No matter. Don't ever say that to me again, or I'll have you de-rezzed."

"I would never be a dirty screw, a backstabbing piece of garbage, a narc, a turncoat, a rat, a—"

Rivka cut him off. "Clevarious, inform the crew that I'll be along presently." She stood and held out her arm. "Shall we?"

"I'd love to. I find your Moonstokle Pie disgusting, but I don't care as long as I don't have to eat it."

"Red eats it just to spite my desire for leftovers."

"Red eats it because he's always hungry. That boy burns a lot of calories."

"And that." They strolled through the corridor to the

nearby galley. With the addition of the boyfriends, it was a full house. Everyone was there, including all the SCAMPs.

Red started waving his hands like a conductor. *"For she's a jolly good fellow, for she's a jolly good fellow…"*

The others joined in.

"What in the holy jump the fuck up and down has possessed you people?" She pointed an accusing finger at Red. "You seem to be the ringleader. Out with it." She crossed her arms and tapped one foot.

"We all took vacation and you didn't for the past couple weeks…"

Rivka held up a hand. "Let me stop you right there. We did. We just didn't tell you party-crashers where we were."

"I told you," Ankh said emotionlessly.

"Where'd you go?"

"Pleasure moon. We got married while we were there," Rivka deadpanned.

"The fuck?" Red blurted. Everyone stared, mouths open. "You got *married*?"

"We did not," Rivka said. She looked at Tyler. "I smell Moonstokle Pie." She bumped her way to the front of the line and took half the pie of her favorite deep-dish pizza.

Ankh eased in behind her and selected his usual fare, but unlike the norm, he took a spot at a galley table. Rivka sat next to him.

"Thanks for your help on this case," she told him and Erasmus.

"We have done nothing except ensure that the planets comply with their signed agreement with the Federation."

Rivka looked around and spoke in a conspiratorial

voice. "But you're tapping their line to Albion, too, aren't you?"

"Not that you know of," Erasmus replied, using Ankh's voice. Ankh's eye twitched as if he were fighting Erasmus, who probably wanted to wink. His avatar did that in the digital universe in which they spent most of their time. Ankh wasn't a winker. The epic battle resulted in Ankh's face contorting and too much blinking. He stood, pushed his plate toward Chrys, and left. She took the plate and followed him out.

Tyler sat down next to her. "That could have been the strangest thing I've ever seen."

Rivka laughed musically. The team was having fun, even Chaz and Dennicron. Red had roped Chaz into a contest of tossing hot wings into the air and catching them in his mouth. A SCAMP's hand-eye coordination was incomparable, except they'd never programmed their reflexes to catch things in their mouths. Chaz did his best, but the wings hit his face until the flesh was stained with hot sauce.

Red roared with laughter. He caught her watching and moved to sit next to her.

"What's up with the party?" Rivka asked.

"One thing you've maintained throughout: no matter how bad things were, we had fun. This one? Screw Frenzik. Look at the planets we've visited so far. Those fuckers *seem* happy."

"We've only talked with the people they've shown us. Maybe we should talk with the general populace."

"It appears that we have time," Red replied.

"I think we're going to find that they're better off. It'll

make any punitive action problematic. My hands might be tied, but Frenzik? He's the only one I want. I don't care about Morbido despite his stupid name."

"I thought it was just me." Red laughed uproariously. He finished abruptly, "I can take him if it comes to that, Magistrate."

"I'm sure you'd like to give it a shot. He's a paper-pusher. He may be tall, but he's soft. I could feel it when I hit him."

"I'm sure you did." Red giggled and re-enacted the uppercut to the groin. "Pow! Right in the goolies."

"Thanks for the party, Red. I'm going back for Round Two. Then I'm going to the gym for a workout. Clear my mind, and first thing in the morning, we'll pound the pavement and see what the average Finx native has to say. Let's get some more information with which to work. In the meantime, we'll keep studying. We need to find his endgame. What is his long-term goal?"

Rivka returned to the counter and loaded her plate once more. She took slices of Red's favorite, double meat with extra cheese, looking at him while she did it.

He threw his hands up. "What the fuck? How about you eat *your* crappy pizza?"

"I've had mine, and now I want yours. But it's not really mine or yours. It's all of ours because we're one team."

"Here we are, trying to do a good thing by being a tight-knit group, and there you are, violating human decency."

The combat team occupied half the room with the pilots and Cole and Clodagh. They snickered and adjusted their seats to get a better view of the inevitable throw-down.

Rivka smiled at them. "You know we call you 'the boyfriends.'"

The three shrugged. Furny spoke for them. "And?"

"And that's it. Is there supposed to be more?"

"Maybe studly boyfriends. Lifesaving-gift-to-the-universe boyfriends. Boyfriends of magnanimous generosity," Cole offered. "*The* boyfriends. It's pretty august. Thank you!" He ended by standing with his arms wide and bowing to the group.

Rivka stuffed half an oversized slice of Red's pizza into her mouth.

Red assumed his best neutral expression. "I am solid as an asteroid hurtling through space at a gazillion kilometers per hour." He struck a pose.

Rivka looked at Tyler for an explanation of the shenanigans.

He whispered in her ear, "If you're stressed, they're stressed. They're trying to keep you from getting angry. Focus on the case. Put the perp in prison. Declare victory and move on."

Rivka went to the front of the room and raised her hands for quiet.

A hot wing appeared out of nowhere and sailed toward her. She caught it deftly and ate it, then wiped her mouth and smiled.

"I appreciate what you're trying to do, and you have accomplished your goal. Frenzik makes me mad, but how can I stay angry when I'm surrounded by such good people? Here's what we're going to do. Sahved is going to lead a team in search of the former ministers to get their statements. Red and I will go ashore to talk with the average person on the street to get their take on the new governmental leadership. The Singularity will monitor the systems in place on Ypswich and here on Finx to make sure these two worlds remain in compliance.

"Finally, but most importantly, Clevarious will maintain a twenty-four seven monitor on the drones. When we see Frenzik raise his ugly head, we're going to pound it down and keep pounding until he outruns his ability to Gate away. That's when we'll disable his ship and secure his Gate drive for study.

"If it contains stolen technology, he'll be going to Jhiordaan. If it's been independently developed, we'll learn that, too. In that case, we'll slap an injunction on him so fast his head will spin. Then the Federation will pass a law making Gate drives on private vessels illegal, subjecting them to confiscation. Frenzik. He's the one we want, and you know what we're going to do? We're going to lock in the good things that Rising Sun Industries is doing. They'll keep doing good things no matter how much it hurts."

Rivka looked at her feet and thought hard but didn't have anything else to say.

Red walked over and gave her a hug. On his way back to his seat, he stole her plate. He faced the Magistrate, and before the gods and the universe, he licked both pizza slices.

CHAPTER EIGHT

***Wyatt Earp*, Finx Capital City, Common Spaceport**
There was a mob at the airlock, waiting for the transports they'd rented for the day. Two vehicles, one for Sahved's group and one for the Magistrate. Sahved was first out with Chaz and Dennicron.

Lindy opted to remain with the Magistrate.

With Chaz's upgraded body, he almost violated the Federation law on warbots. Rivka had made him remove his rocket-launching saddlebags, to his dismay and Sahved's appreciation.

Red and Lindy were armed and wore ballistic protection under heavy coats. If they were going to walk the streets, they had to protect themselves against the weather. Rivka wore a sweater beneath her Magistrate's jacket. She also carried Reaper, her neutron pulse weapon.

Three geared up for war, and three outfitted for innocuous information-gathering.

Sahved waved for the SCAMPs to follow when the high-topped van arrived. They hurried into it, and the vehicle quickly departed. Sahved waved from inside, but he couldn't tell if the Magistrate saw him do so.

Their first stop was the local police station to get the addresses of the former ministers. The driver would know how to get there, and Chaz and Dennicron would know if he was trying to pull something underhanded.

"You have a beautiful city. Very refreshing," Sahved said to the driver, attempting the small talk that humans seemed to excel at.

"Of course. It is Finx. Finx is beautiful. That's what the word means. This is the land of beauty," the driver replied.

Sahved stared out the front window, at a loss for the proper response. He finally spoke after an uncomfortably long silence. "Thank you."

That didn't make it any better. Chaz moved in. "Do you have any videos here that are uniquely Finx? We'd love to watch some of the local fare. Federation vids can be so staid."

The driver got excited. "There's a series in its second season of one hundred episodes called *Bangers and Trash* about a gang war right here in the city! It's spectacular."

"We'll have to put it on the screen. Should we start with the first episode of the first season?"

"Absolutely. You'll be hooked right away like the rest of us."

Chaz leaned closer. "Is it based on real events?"

The driver laughed. "Not at all. We don't have that problem like other planets. Finx natives aren't susceptible to drug highs. There's no alcohol on the planet except for the tourists who come to enjoy the beauty, but they're better off if they learn to do without."

"You watch a fictional story about your hometown?" Chaz was confused.

"Aren't all stories fiction? Unless you're watching the news, of course."

Chaz leaned back since they were approaching the police headquarters. "I agree. Thank you. *Bangers and Trash*. We'll get on it as soon as possible."

"I'll be right here," the driver happily called through the open door after the three had climbed out of the van. Sahved waved. It was his standard "Goodbye, see you later."

Chaz clapped him on the back. "You have the lead, my friend."

"Do you really watch videos?" Sahved asked on their way to the station's front door.

"At a hundred times the speed. We consume a huge amount of media as part of our training to better understand the meat wagons. I mean, the warmbloods, I mean, you guys."

"I understand," Sahved said with a small laugh. "I can't digest it that quickly. I'm still buried in my legal studies. I have a long way to go."

"It's not easy. Federation law is nothing like what you have on Yemilore. You're learning a whole new system from the ground up, complete with centuries of precedent and nuance. I'd say that we mastered the law in minutes, but we haven't because there's one thing you possess that we do not, and that's your gut. You feel things from the shades of gray suspects and witnesses provide in their interviews. You connect dots that are not logically connected because it makes sense to your intuitive mind. We are trying to overcome that hurdle. Until we do, we cannot be trusted to move into a Magistrate's position."

"A Magistrate! I never fancied myself as one. I don't think I could inflict punishment. I can be the investigator, the judge, and the jury, but I could not be the executioner."

"Then we shall have to remain partners in this venture," Dennicron offered.

They entered the police headquarters, and like most smaller planets with minimal crime, there weren't many law enforcement officials. They found a desk officer and one other. They couldn't tell who was in charge due to the lack of distinctive uniforms.

"We're from the office of the Magistrate and need a list of addresses for the former ministers. The ones who have seemingly gone missing," Sahved began evenly. He made no accusations.

"They resigned. They're private citizens. They can do what they want." The officer made no move to pull any information from his computer.

"I have a search warrant." Sahved waved a datapad.

"Harassing private citizens. Is that really how you want to make your mark on Finx?" one of the officers asked.

"I have a warrant. It's not harassment if it's in response to a valid charge."

"What's the charge?"

"Misadventure." Sahved stared with his best blank expression, the one he had learned from Ankh.

"Your Federation laws are bizarre. I'm glad I'm not responsible for enforcing them."

Sahved smiled and twirled his fingers. "You aren't, but

we are. We need that information, please, so we may continue our investigation."

"Fine. Give me a minute to pull it up." He glanced at Chaz and Dennicron, who would have been far more efficient pulling the information from the system. Sahved watched the SCAMPs' eyes stare into the distance. He assumed they were accessing the police systems but didn't want to know. The SIs were stretching their legs to the border of legality and beyond.

He justified it by the latitude the Magistrate enjoyed to stop the Federation's worst crimes and worst criminals. Their crimes affected huge swaths of the population. They needed to be taken off the street. Most times, the perp was known. They only had to gather the evidence to make the conviction watertight.

In this instance, they were building a case against Frenzik. By speaking to the ministers, they'd learn the extent of the subterfuge. How did Frenzik make them look so bad that they resigned en masse?

In two minutes, the officer handed Sahved a printed list. Eight of the ten ministers were on it. "What about the other two?"

"We have no information for them," the officer replied.

"They were ministers, leaders of your government. How could you have no information on them?"

"Do you think he's judging us? I feel like he's judging us." The officer never took his eyes off the Yemilorian. "They resigned and left the planet. We have neither the responsibility nor the resources to track everyone who used to live on Finx. I expect you have the resources, so why don't you spin up your own group to do your work for you?"

"This didn't have to be unpleasant," Sahved told the officer. He spun his fingers in the air, not because he was anxious but because he was agitated. "We're only doing our job, following lines of inquiry until we get to the perpetrator."

"They resigned. There is no crime. They were absolute garbage. Maybe you can punch them in the face when you see them. Do it for me since I'm far too professional to do it. That would make us happy if you are looking to make amends."

Sahved shook his head. "I have nothing to make amends for. I'm only doing my job, just like you. Aren't you on the clock? So very much punching the clock and working. If we weren't here, what else would you be doing?"

"We have a lot to do, plus the latest episode of *Bangers* just came out."

"Ah, yes! *Bangers and Trash*. We're big fans. Who'd believe drug crime in the city?" Sahved asked.

"Not us," the officer declared with a big smile, his demeanor very different.

"We'll leave you to it, then. Enjoy the episode." Sahved waved and ducked through the door to get outside. Chaz and Dennicron followed. The van was where it had dropped them off, a short walk away.

"They love their show," Chaz said. "We look forward to watching it."

Sahved tapped Chaz on the arm. "Look for subliminal messaging. It is strange that everyone is smitten in the same way. It's not natural."

"You picked that up from the two conversations?" Chaz asked.

"I did. It's off. A gut feeling, as you said."

"We have so much to learn. We were happy to find common ground with the video but saw that as a social victory, not a link to the investigation."

Sahved shrugged. "It may not be, but it's a lead. They've pacified this entire population. Did they do it solely through good deeds? I doubt that."

"You are a very good investigator." Chaz clapped lightly. "For the Magistrate, we're going to nail Frenzik."

Rivka's vehicle looked identical to the one that took Sahved's team. They boarded and asked the driver to take them to a general location in the city. A place where people would be walking the streets. The common citizen. The driver was amused. He turned up the music to forestall further conversation, even though Rivka wanted to get his take, too.

She tapped him on the shoulder.

He turned the music down.

"What do you think of the new prime minister and the direction Finx is going?" Rivka kept her hand on his shoulder. Despite the Finx being humanoid, their thought patterns were different from humans'. She could only make out general emotions. Regarding the new governmental leadership, he was positive. Almost overwhelmingly so.

"It is good. People have food and credits again. I am happy to return to work. I like what I do." He spoke in clipped phrases, a method learned as a driver who couldn't maintain a longer conversation.

She thanked him. She'd "heard" everything she needed to hear.

When they arrived at a busy area downtown, the driver stopped. "I'll wait for you here."

They climbed out. Red and Lindy slung their railguns across their backs to be less obvious, but they still stood out since they were larger than the natives. They also wore body armor and carried weapons. Many shied away from the Magistrate until Red and Lindy gave her more space, to Red's chagrin. His trigger finger twitched in anticipation of being needed. He kept his hand on his railgun, ready to pull it to its firing position.

Rivka waved and smiled cordially. "May I speak with you for a moment?" She blocked a native's way until the female agreed to talk. "What do you think of the new prime minister?"

"I think he's just fine," the Finx native replied. "Good, even. Look, I'm going to be late to my new job, so please…"

The female's eyes pleaded with Rivka, who stepped aside and thanked her for her help.

The rest of the engagements throughout the morning were the same. Busy people who liked being busy and could spare no time for a casual conversation.

Rivka leaned against a nearby wall, with Red and Lindy flanking her. "Everybody loves Morbido, or at least they love the results of Rising Sun investments and opportunities."

"Is it worth your time to stay here?" Lindy asked.

"That's the million-credit question." Rivka watched more locals walk past. They were happy enough. No one looked miserable or down on their luck. "You're probably right. We haven't wasted our time. We've confirmed that Frenzik has gotten better at hiding his ulterior motive, which we have not discovered. I don't think we will while we're here. What we need is to find where he went. We need to find *him*."

"What about the ministers?"

"They'll be alive, I suspect. They'll probably tell stories about how they were blackmailed for their incompetence or insider trading or something unsavory. Unsuccessful leaders have a tendency to pad their own nests first. That's what makes Frenzik's moves even more puzzling. How does he convince these planets to turn over everything to him? I am utterly besnoggled by it all. He's not a philanthropist, not in any way, shape, or form."

"Then you need to talk with him. Let's get the comm links installed. He'll raise his ugly head. I guarantee he's getting antsy. He's not quite the hiding type," Red offered.

"Let's return to the ship." Rivka had seen what she needed to see. Her answers weren't on Finx. "Belay that. Let's go to the prime minister's office. I want to compliment him on what he's done for the natives of Finx."

They had to wake the driver when they returned to the van. He didn't care where he took them since he was booked for the day.

The prime minister was in. They'd kept him away from his duties for too long the previous day. Rivka found little pleasure in the revelation.

Judging by Morbido's face, he was not pleased to see

Rivka. He didn't welcome her. He sat rigidly in the oversized chair at his oversized desk.

"We'll call this an outbrief. I want to thank you for your hospitality. I'll apologize for yesterday's brusqueness. Your process is delivering results that matter for the natives. They are happy. Keep doing what you're doing. I'll make no threats or warnings. I appreciate the results. That's about all we can do, isn't it?"

"I appreciate your apology, Magistrate. Having explored the option of filing charges against you for assault and battery, I found a mountain in my way. Seems Magistrates are untouchable. I *will* ask that you not do it again. Although you may find my size intimidating, I am not a fighter."

Red snorted. Rivka silenced him with a look while biting her lip to keep from laughing.

"I thought you said you were going to let it go, but I expected such duplicity. We could talk about your attempt to use your size to intimidate me by looming over me, which didn't work out in your favor whatsoever. Maybe you're so used to looming that it comes naturally, but that's neither here nor there. I think you know better than to try it again on anyone. There we are. We'll take our leave of Finx. Please don't do anything to force me to come back."

"See?" The Albion leaned back in his chair until it creaked in protest and folded his hands over his midriff. "You can't help yourself but to threaten people. Your existence must be a sad one indeed. If you'll excuse me, I have a great deal of work to catch up on."

Rivka didn't rise to the bait. "According to Finx law,

you have two days to fill the ministerial positions. Do you have the new candidates selected?"

Morbido looked smug. "They'll be arriving from Albion tomorrow."

"Great! *Rising Sun* will return. We'll wait in orbit for it, then. I have questions for the ship's captain."

Morbido clenched his teeth, angry both at Rivka and himself.

Rivka waved over her shoulder as she walked away.

Red glared at Morbido until the door closed.

CHAPTER NINE

***Wyatt Earp*, in Orbit over Finx**

"We only interviewed three of the ministers," Sahved complained. It was more of a mild annoyance since he wasn't allowed to fulfill his tasks before he was recalled to the ship.

"And you found exactly what I expected," Rivka replied. "I understand that we want to be thorough in all things, but this isn't where we need to focus our efforts. The challenge is coming from Albion, and his name is Frenzik. Our case hinges on intercepting him."

"Do you think he'll come?" Sahved asked. Skepticism filled his face.

"No. I expect the Singularity has heard a frantic call from Morbido to Albion instructing them not to bring *Rising Sun*." Rivka looked up. "Clevarious, would there be anything in the airwaves that suggests Frenzik has been called off?"

"I'm reluctant to admit that we know he was never

coming. They are taking private transport, but here's one name that might screw you into the overhead."

Rivka clenched her jaw and steeled herself. "Who's coming?"

"Ahsooleyman and Belloward."

"What the hell happened? How are they out of Jhiordaan? I put them in there for seven years."

"Petition to the Federation Council. The ambassadors wanted to make a good impression on the leadership in the Barrier Nebula," Clevarious explained. "Lance Reynolds argued rather vociferously against it, but he was a minority voice."

"We're putting a convicted felon in charge of the good people of Finx. A guy who duped those he was in charge of to play them against each other in support of turning the population into slaves. That Assholeman. We're talking the same guy, aren't we?"

"It's embarrassing, Magistrate. Those bleeding hearts!" The SI managed a good crescendo with his statement.

"They're trying to do their best by the Federation, but they don't know that when we're talking about the twelve planets of the Barrier Nebula, we're talking Malpace Frenzik. There is no one else. This suggests he has far more influence in the Council than we know. How could anyone champion such a thing without me hearing about it?"

Sahved shook his head. "Lance Reynolds knew. He could have told the High Chancellor, who should have passed it to you. It would have been nice to know that you'll see those two again. I don't want to see them. They are bad people."

"Just this once, Sahved, you have understated the situation. They are very bad people. Putting them in charge of sectors of society can't be a good idea. The one thing they have is absolute loyalty to Frenzik. They went down for him. This is their reward, but what does that look like? Why Finx? There's nothing here except a little raw material. Are they investing the time and effort in clearing house for mineral rights? I wouldn't put it past Frenzik, but is the deposit that rich?"

"They are minerals in high demand. It will be quite lucrative," Clevarious replied.

"The big winner in the resource extraction game. A bunch of Finx moving up to middle class while Frenzik and his cronies become fabulously wealthy," Sahved groused.

"That's not a crime, but I sympathize with you. Raising people out of poverty is the initial success. People should be able to continue improving their lives, but once again, that's my opinion. It is not supported by evidence detailing a crime. Maybe the natives of Finx will rise up against their Rising Sun masters."

"They seem to like their Rising Sun saviors," Sahved replied. "Very much so. It is a bromance of galactic proportions. We also discovered that they all love a new show called *Bangers and Trash*. Chaz and Dennicron are watching all the episodes to determine if there's a subliminal message contained within that makes the natives more susceptible to suggestions. It is the bizarrest thing I have ever seen in all my days."

"There's the Sahved we love," Rivka said. "Excellent work." She chewed her lip. "The new pack of ministers is coming on a commercial flight and will be here tomorrow."

"And they are all Albions," Clevarious clarified.

"As we suspected. We have oversight in place on the comm lines, do we not?"

"I can neither confirm nor deny that such a thing is in place."

"As you wish. Keep me apprised if and when they show their real objective. As a matter of fact, because of the usurpation of power on Finx, I will issue a short-term search warrant for communications between Finx and Albion. That reminds me; I better send a private note to the queen."

Rivka left the conference room and hurried across the corridor to her quarters.

She brought up her hologrid and scrawled a quick message to the queen to be sent as an image.

I hope you're doing well today, Queen. Your monarchy remains strong. Keep working with the prime minister, but watch him closely for usurping your power and pillaging your planet. In the short term, things may look good, but the monarchy has stood strong for centuries, and it will for centuries to come. The Finx will need you to save them.

"Bingo!" Clevarious shouted throughout *Wyatt Earp*. "*Rising Sun* has just Gated into orbit over Albion."

Rivka jumped off her chair and ran for the bridge, shouting, "Spin us up for a jump to Albion. The game is afoot!"

"The game is space-chase," Clevarious corrected. "I don't see how it can be a foot. Gate drive is energizing."

"Cole! Get your team ready for EVA." Extra-vehicular activity. Boarding a hostile ship. They were going to seize *Rising Sun* and everyone within. "Power up the EMP weapon."

Rivka slowed to a walk and strolled onto the bridge.

"I see he waited until the moment the ship arrived at the Finx Gate with the new ministers. C, the Singularity didn't hear anything about Frenzik's movements?"

Clevarious confirmed, "He is using a channel that is unavailable to us."

"Maybe that was his push to keep SIs out of the system. With an organization like his, he has to move huge amounts of data. Coordination is key because he handles the logistics support for these planets flawlessly."

The Gate formed in front of the ship, and *Wyatt Earp* slipped through.

Given the data from the drone, they arrived within ten kilometers of Frenzik's ship. "Give me a channel, please." Rivka requested.

Clodagh gestured when the channel was live.

"Heave to and prepare to be boarded," Rivka said.

"Magistrate! Look at you, all the way out here. I'd love to stay, but we have places to go and people to see."

"Energy surge. Gate drive is coming online."

"Get an angle where we can see through it to know where he's going." Rivka leaned forward in the captain's chair until she was almost standing.

A Gate formed in front of *Rising Sun*. It was a different shade and had a different sheen than Federation Gates. Her stomach roiled at the thought of him having a "legal" Gate drive.

"Gather data on that Gate, too, while it's up," Rivka said. "Prepare to Gate."

They watched Frenzik's ship slip through. The Gate sparkled until it closed.

"He's gone to Hergin," Clevarious said. "Confirmed by the drone."

Before Rivka could order it, the Gate formed in front of *Wyatt Earp*.

"Prepare a beacon that we can attach to his ship. By my count, we have a solid thirty seconds to fly by and launch an emitter into his ship."

"Working it now," Clevarious replied. "It won't be ready for this engagement."

Wyatt Earp slipped over the event horizon to a point aft of *Rising Sun* and accelerated to within a kilometer.

"Malpace," Rivka began casually, "I'd like to talk with you about your future and the future of Rising Sun Industries. You can keep running until you burn out your Gate drive. Then the only one who will be there to save you is me. Maybe I'll decide that letting your ship drift into a nearby star is best for all of us."

"Nothing wrong with my ship, Magistrate. It's just starting to get its feet under it for the long haul. I'm surprised that you're able to track us through the Gate. I didn't think that was possible."

"With faith, all things are possible. I'm going to need you to heave to and shut down your engines. We'll be along presently."

"You know I can't do that. You've had a hard-on for me for the past year. I don't like being stampeded. You Magistrates have too much power. The council is revisiting your authority. Seems I'm not the only one with concerns."

"Only cockroaches fear the light, Malpace. Innocent until proven guilty, although you're making it easy to find you guilty of at least failing to heed a lawful order to submit to examination regarding your Gate drive. Military technology is covered under nonproliferation laws. If you've developed it separately, then you would be the only one, so the legal presumption is that you've stolen the technology. It rates a search warrant. All legal. All above board for probable cause. The case is made. I said, heave to."

"Energy building," Clevarious reported. "In position."

Wyatt Earp moved so close to *Rising Sun* that it could have gone through the Gate with Frenzik's ship, but that was a higher risk than Rivka wanted to take. If the Gate closed on them, they'd all be killed.

"Ypswich," Clevarious said. "Drone confirms."

The Gate formed in front of Rivka's ship. "How was the energy spike this time? Any signs that the repeated jumps are taking a toll?"

"Identical readings from the first Gate. I'm sorry, Magistrate."

"Nothing to be sorry for, C. We'll eventually hit him with the EMP weapon. Maybe now would be a good time for that unless we can hit his Gate drive with a shot from the railgun."

"The Gate drive is in the middle of the ship. We'd have to blow the ship apart to hit it. I do not recommend that," Clodagh interjected.

"Let's keep the collateral damage to a minimum. I want Frenzik behind bars, not blasted into space dust."

Wyatt Earp joined *Rising Sun* in orbit over Ypswich.

"This grows tiresome, Frenzik. Heave to. Last warning."

"I don't think I'll do that," Frenzik replied. "None of the conditions for my heaving to, as you say, have changed. I need some guarantees before I have a face-to-face conversation with you."

"Keep talking. At this point, it's a conversation. In the near future, it'll be a suspect interview, and if you keep running, it'll become an interrogation. Your friends in the council won't be able to save you. It's just us out here on the frontier."

"Energy is spiking. There is a warble!" Clevarious declared.

Rivka didn't know what that meant, but different was good. Her plan to run Frenzik down was working.

The main screen clouded as *Wyatt Earp* closed on Frenzik's ship. "What's going on?"

"They've flooded space with chaff behind their vessel."

"Fire the beacon! Get something on that ship."

"Beacon away," Clodagh replied.

The Gate formed, and *Rising Sun* blasted through with a trail of chaff behind it. When the Gate closed, Rivka waited for confirmation from Clevarious.

"Tell me the beacon attached." Rivka didn't sound hopeful.

"It did not. The chaff affected it. Those metal strips kept it from zeroing in since it has a magnetic coupler. The ship has not shown up around any of the populated planets of the Nebula Barrier."

Rivka didn't say it out loud, but the message pounded inside her brain. *We lost him.*

"I'll be in Engineering, talking to Ambassador Erasmus." Rivka strolled out.

The formal term was the clarification that she wanted something from the Singularity.

In Engineering, which was also the embassy of the Singularity, she found Ankh embroiled within a hologrid that had grown so dense that she could barely see through it. She did what she always did. She plunged through the light show and squeezed inside with Ankh.

She was transported into the digital world in which Ankh and Erasmus did most of their work.

Erasmus doffed his top hat and bowed deeply to welcome Rivka back to their domain.

Ankh's head was grossly oversized, but he walked around effortlessly since the avatar's head had no weight.

"We're very busy, Magistrate," Ankh said.

"So, business as usual. I'll be brief."

Before Rivka could say another word, Ankh threw his avatar's T-Rex arms in the air and laughed uproariously. His head shrank to normal size. "That'll be a first."

"I'm always brief!" Rivka jammed her avatar's fists into her hips and adopted her best belligerent look.

Erasmus appeared beside her. He draped a warm arm over her shoulders. "We know. Ankh was just being mean since I was in the middle of completely destroying him in chess. He's a bit put out."

"Why is your arm warm?" Rivka wondered. They were in the digital space. Physical sensations like hot and cold weren't the norm.

"Ah! You like that?" Erasmus stepped away. "Is it cooler now?"

Her feet were uncomfortable. She looked down to find she was barefoot and standing on ice. While she looked, the view changed to a black, featureless floor. Her boots were on.

Rivka shrugged off the pair's assault on her senses. "Who are the ambassadors in the council that Frenzik has in his pocket?"

"A challenging question because there are so many ambassadors. We don't listen in on their conversations. Usually, that is."

"But you know who filed the motions on Frenzik's behalf and then who they met with as part of their public calendars, sorted according to time to create a linkage of probable and possible contacts. These ambassadors may not know who they're doing business with. I want to know who they are, first, and second, what he has over them."

"What if he has nothing on them except the promise to do something? The raw materials he's already started extracting from Finx need a bidding war to get the most for them. Frenzik has floated such an exchange."

"Who is bidding?" Rivka asked.

"Those records are confidential." Erasmus smiled and winked. He used his walking stick to point at the wall, which turned into a scrolling list of names and the planets they represented.

"You are gods of the information age," Rivka cooed.

"We put the 'I' in information," Erasmus replied.

"You weren't destroying me," Ankh muttered.

"The claim of a true competitor!" Erasmus howled. "Is there anything else you need, Magistrate?"

"You've provided everything I asked for with expeditious joy." Rivka waved since she intended to leave the digital realm.

"That's Ankh and me, the purveyors of joy. We are pleased to assist. When will we stop by Efrahim? There are indications that they would like to hire an SI, but that is solely on a back-channel to Yoll, transmitted by a freighter after it left the planet."

Rivka nodded. "Sounds like our next stop is to install a comm link on Efrahim. What do you know about those people?"

"They are very much like Crenellians but with four arms and extremely short, only a meter tall. A humorless green-skinned people. Maybe they are less like Crenellians than I first noted. In any case, we have a candidate, Trevazlifarmington, who we'll submit for consideration."

"Tree is welcome to join them. Not that you need my approval, but I love seeing more SIs helping planets manage themselves into prosperity."

"If they would only listen to us more. Alas, it is our lot in life to give advice that goes unheeded." Erasmus held his hand over his heart and sighed.

"I'll leave you to it, then. Time to hit the road."

"Are we landing?" Ankh asked.

"No. Why would you think that?"

"Hitting the road. There are no roads in space, so I must assume that we are going where there are roads."

"We are not. The road is ephemeral—the road to the stars. We'll spin up the Gate and be at Efrahim as soon as I can get the team ready."

"Chaz and Dennicron are already packing the equipment and tools," Erasmus replied. "Clevarious has made the calculations. We'll be at Efrahim before you can say Bob's your uncle but not Billy Bob and most definitely not Billy Joe Jim Bob."

"Why would I want to say that?" Rivka finished her question outside the hologrid and blinked herself back to the physical world. She took a small step to make sure her balance was solid before hurrying from the engineering section.

Red was waiting for her by the airlock. "Clevarious said we're going ashore at Efrahim. Aren't those the little green weirdos?"

"That's not how I'd say it, but yes. Efrahim, here we come."

"We're already here, Magistrate, with priority clearance on the transit corridor from space to the surface," Clevarious reported.

"Now, that's how you treat a lady." Rivka stuck her nose in the air.

Tyler strolled around the corner carrying her jacket. "C said you'd need this."

"I'm hanging on for this ride. Have you ever been inside with Erasmus and Ankh?"

"That is hallowed ground I dare not tread upon," Tyler replied. "Can I go ashore with you? I've got cabin fever something fierce."

CHAPTER TEN

***Wyatt Earp*, Efrahim Spaceport**
"They look like bugs," Red observed as he looked through the airlock's porthole.

"The race is the Efrahimi. It's probably their four arms that's a little disconcerting," Rivka replied. "We have work to do. Let's meet our hosts."

Red blocked the Magistrate from leaving the ship first. He smiled down at her.

"You're looking a little pudgy," Rivka taunted.

He lost his grin. "Somebody is going to get his ass kicked for it, too."

"It's for hydration, dumbass. You carry a little pudge so I don't have to carry a big goon."

"I'm never going to live that down."

"Three times, Red. I don't want there to be any more. You don't want any more episodes. Your internal water tank will keep you from collapsing."

"But it makes me look fat."

"It makes you look healthy."

Red popped the outer hatch and stepped through. A stiff breeze cut through his clothes to his bare skin. He breathed in deeply and exhaled slowly. "I hear this is good fat-man weather. Probably cold for you light-weights," Red called through the hatch as he continued down the ramp.

The rest of the team followed. The small vehicle that waited for them suggested they'd need another two like it or one much bigger vehicle.

Red shook his head and stormed up to the small group that waited for them. Before he could speak, Rivka tapped his arm, and he stepped aside.

"Thank you for meeting me. This is my first trip to Efrahim. I'm Magistrate Rivka Anoa, and I'd like to talk with your Supreme Leader."

"He is expecting you. Do you have the communications gear and SI?"

"We will install the new communications equipment to bring Efrahim into compliance with the Federation charter. As for contracting with an SI, I'll leave that to Ambassadors Erasmus and Ankh."

The Crenellian stepped forward. "We have a candidate. His name is Trevazlifarmington, but he goes by Tree."

"I'm sure any candidate you put forward will be more than adequate. We look forward to running him through the system to check for compatibility and receiving any short-term recommendations he may have for optimization."

"We'll review the contract. Please transmit it to the Singularity."

The Efrahimi produced a small computer and tapped

through a series of screens before closing the device. "Sent," he declared.

"We have received your request, job listing, and proposed contract. We'll review it immediately. Please open your system, and we'll facilitate the movement of your candidate from the embassy."

"It is open. Access code is in the request letter," the Efrahimi replied.

Rivka stood and watched, fascinated by the efficiency of the effort. The entire transaction would take less than two minutes.

Ankh's expression had remained neutral the entire time, as usual. He didn't get excited, unlike in the digital world. There, he was far more emotional, albeit negative. His victories were of the cerebral type, but they didn't send him into excessive celebrations.

The leader of the reception committee turned his attention to Rivka. "We welcome Magistrate Rivka to Efrahim. We have prepared a banquet in your honor."

"Why, thank you. That's pleasant. My team needs to install communications equipment to give Efrahim a direct link to Yoll as required under the Federation charter. I have a writ of mandamus, so you're covered with anyone who might take exception to the new capability."

"There won't be anyone like that. We look forward to returning to a state of compliance with the Federation."

Rivka reached out a hand, but the Efrahimi didn't take it. The group moved into the small vehicle, leaving Rivka and her team standing there. Presently, a bus pulled up. There was barely enough room for Rivka, two bodyguards, three SCAMPs, a Crenellian, and a Yemilorian. Tyler was left on the outside looking in. They ducked to get inside. Sahved crouched to squeeze into the doorway but got no farther inside.

Tyler waved. "I'm gonna pass on this one. You kids have fun."

Red grunted from where he was compacted into a too-small seat. "Suck my balls."

The bus followed the tiny car. They wound their way through a miniature city with no buildings above three stories. The highest was barely over Sahved's head.

"Fantastic," Rivka muttered, watching the buildings go by. "They live and work close to the ground."

"Chaz and Dennicron, the leadership team is missing here, too, right? What does that look like?"

Chaz replied, "A ruling advisorship of five. They have disappeared. The Supreme Leader has been left on his own."

"The structure and titles are similar to Ypswich's," Rivka noted.

"Ypswich is the nearest planet to Efrahim. That's where the influence comes from," Dennicron said. "The advisorship group went on a retreat and never returned."

"We need to find them. We'll use *Wyatt Earp's* sensors to scan the area and collect what information we can, from where they were last seen to where they were going."

"Do you wish the ship to undertake that task now?" Dennicron asked.

Rivka didn't have to think for long. "Do it. The ship can pick us up wherever we may be. Tell them to cloak during their search. No one needs to see the ship."

Dennicron transmitted the order.

"This group seems more welcoming," Red said. He had hunched over to look out the window.

"They weren't in as dire of shape as Finx. I'm not sure they were in bad shape at all, but you know what they have in excess?" Rivka asked.

Chaz and Dennicron knew. Ankh didn't care. He had detached from the conversations. He was also the only one who was seated comfortably.

Rivka continued, "Massive swaths of arable land with the opportunity to produce enough food to satisfy two more planets. This is the most fertile planet in the Barrier Nebula. Frenzik is a master of strategic supply. He is going to dominate everything that matters. He's not buying up convenience stores. He's not buying any outlets. He's controlling the supply chains. It's a monopoly of galactic proportions, but it's not illegal to dominate the supply chain. It *is* illegal to manipulate the planetary leadership to gain control. Exactly like we saw on Ypswich and Lewbamar."

"On Ypswich, they took over sewage management. I'm not seeing the exportability," Red said.

"The one who controls the utilities controls the population. Turn off the electricity or the water and see how fast society degenerates. Turn it on, and see how fast they love their saviors."

"Would the Ypsicanti love an Albion?"

"Not at all," Rivka replied. "But they would love another Ypsicanti. That's why they didn't insert an Albion. I'm looking at Ypswich and Lewbamar as training for their big move. They disappeared from sight for a few months before raising their ugly heads again. On Finx, they removed the opposition leadership through exposure and blackmail. Here, who knows how they removed the advisorship? That leaves Hergin and Glazoron. We need to find out how those leadership groups were removed. And we need a complete workup on what Rising Sun Industries is after on those planets."

Chaz raised a finger to shoulder height. He was bent over double in his seat. "Hergin is minerals, and Glazoron is high-tech manufacture. Together, Hergin and Glazoron can build Gate drives."

"That is disturbing," Rivka replied. She chewed her cheek while the bus trundled on, stuffed floor to ceiling with Rivka's team. She ducked her head to look out the window. Under different circumstances, she would have found the architecture to be fantastic and beautiful in a Lilliputian way. The city sprawled, but they had space to expand laterally. There was no need to explore a vertical arrangement.

Factories to process the raw foods were positioned along the outskirts of the town. The labor force lived in the city but traveled out to the fields and farms during the day. Agriculture dominated on Efrahim. It wasn't looked down on as a profession. Workers from tech factories had the harder road to travel to convince their friends they were doing something important.

The seat of government was centrally located in the city and was subject to significant criticism since they weren't close to the agricultural centers. Their argument was that by being centrally located, they weren't showing favoritism toward one farm over another. All the fields were equally distant.

Rivka accepted where they were. She didn't care why as long as she had access.

The bus stopped, and the door opened. Sahved fell out backward and rolled around on the ground until he could straighten his legs to get his knees under him. The others extricated themselves in an uncoordinated clown-car way, popping out of the vehicle like corks being yanked out of bottles.

They stood on the sidewalk, stretching to get blood back into their limbs. The SCAMPs watched emotionlessly. Ankh strolled off the vehicle with his nose in the air.

"Somebody was right at home," Red said, not looking at Ankh. His eyes roamed the local area for threats to the Magistrate. The center of the city wasn't busy. There was no reason for the Efrahimi to be here. It wasn't a factory or a center of commerce, and it wasn't a farm, either. It was the anti-city.

Rivka headed inside using a door to the side of the main entrance after Red got stuck in the rotating door. Lindy stayed with the Magistrate while Red attempted to dislodge himself. Chrys came to his rescue. He looked like he was willing to shoot the door off its spindle, but the SI stopped him. Ankh went through the main door. All the others used the door Rivka had used.

Inside, they found her talking to a uniformed officer who looked different from the rest.

Rivka turned to her team. "Let me introduce you to Kalli Effir. She's the chief of law enforcement and our escort while we're here. For those installing the new communication equipment and checking up on Tree's progress, you'll go with Kalli's deputy. The rest of us will meet with the Supreme Leader."

Effir led them down a long hallway. Rivka smiled. Of course the Supreme Leader's office was on the ground floor. The Efrahimi didn't like heights.

The Supreme Leader was an unprepossessing individual, dressed like the others and not pretentious. He stood up to face the influx of people who had to appear as giants to the diminutive Efrahimi. He waved all four hands by way of greeting.

"You must be Magistrate Rivka Anoa," he said, glancing from face to face since he was unsure who was the right person.

Rivka stepped forward. "That's me, indeed. The rest of my team is installing your direct communications link to Yoll. You'll enjoy unfiltered and unencumbered communication with the Federation."

"You don't know what a relief that is. I've been asking for help, but no one ever comes except from Rising Sun Industries. I had to send a message on a freighter to get in touch with the Federation."

"We appreciate your ingenuity. Who cut your comm channels?"

"Rising Sun Industries. Our system started breaking and became harder and harder to fix. They replaced our equipment at no cost as part of a deal to expand their embassy," the Supreme Leader replied.

"But that wasn't enough, was it?"

The Supreme Leader groaned and shook his head. He remained standing. Rivka glanced around to find there were no chairs in the office besides the one behind his desk.

"The Albion wanted more, and then the advisorship disappeared. I've told them no, but I fear for my life."

That pulled in one hundred percent of Rivka's attention. "Do you have any evidence it was Rising Sun Industries threatening you?" She held her breath.

"It was a feeling. Calls at odd times. Pressure. Allegations of taking bribes. More. It was all made up, but they were trying to get me to sign over the planet's leadership to Albion representatives. That's ridiculous because our constitution requires all leaders to be born of Efrahimi parents."

"They probably didn't mean the title, which they intended to be more titular in authority. Rising Sun Industries wanted to call the shots, I expect. Who is putting the pressure on you?"

"That would be an Albion named Penrod. Penrod Frenzik."

Rivka looked at Chaz. "Is that a brother, uncle, son?"

Chaz shook his head. *I don't know. Frenzik's history has never been available to us. He has a hard block on the data, a firewall that our combined efforts have not been able to breach.* He used their internal comm chips to maintain privacy.

Red rolled his jaw and tried to clear his ears, stuffing a finger into his ear canal to clean out whatever seemed to block his hearing.

Rivka looked at Lindy, who shrugged in reply. Rivka returned her attention to the Supreme Leader. "I believe there's a solid link to the CEO of Rising Sun. We've begun a search for the advisorship. Do you have anything besides what you've already sent us?"

"Our people have made no progress. They left for an offsite at the soybean farm northeast and never arrived."

"Somewhere between here and there, they were intercepted. Did you record all air traffic from that day? Please allow our investigators Chaz and Dennicron access to your systems."

"Anything you need, Rivka." The Supreme Leader made a call from his desk and instructed someone on the other end to give Rivka and her team access.

Chaz and Dennicron excused themselves and left the office.

"What makes you so opposed to Rising Sun Industries gaining a foothold on Efrahim? Some of the other planets welcomed them with open arms, tossing them the keys to the castle upon their arrival. You adamantly oppose them, which is refreshing."

The Supreme Leader would have laughed if the Efrahimi showed emotion. "We are able to rule ourselves. We are able to handle our own issues, and we are capable of increasing production to be a net exporter of foodstuffs. The only thing preventing us from doing this? Shipping. Freighters. Rising Sun has cut us off from the freighters. They aren't even open to charging exorbitant rates. They want production control, which leads into export control. To get that, I suspect they've eliminated the advisorship to get me to agree to their demands."

"I will ask that you don't," Rivka said candidly. "Fight them with every fiber of your being. I feel like Efrahim is in good hands. We'll search for the advisorship. We'll get a hold of this Frenzik Number Two and get to the bottom of the borderline harassment."

"I appreciate anything you can do to get Rising Sun Industries off Efrahim." The Supreme Leader bowed slightly.

"What kind of penetration do they have into your planetary resources?"

"They provided the technology after our communications systems broke down. They've also purchased two smaller farms. We blocked them from a bigger purchase, one of our major producers. That's when bad things started to happen, but we couldn't get them out of our comm system. They were sealed and locked from external interference. We couldn't replace them without buying a whole new suite, and you know who runs interplanetary freight."

"Rising Sun Industries has the death grip on freight into and out of Efrahim. They control it throughout the Barrier Nebula." Rivka was surprised and impressed by the Supreme Leader's engagement at the strategic level. He was trying to hold it together when those at lower levels were probably the ones who let Rising Sun get in the door. The Supreme Leader had seen Frenzik for what he was and was fighting to keep Efrahim from becoming another conquest.

"We'll keep your office informed as our investigation progresses."

The comm system is online, Magistrate, Chrys reported from the communications room.

"And," Rivka continued, "your direct link to Yoll is online. You won't have to coopt a friendly freighter captain to send your message outside of official channels. I wonder if Frenzik knows he's got captains going outside the company? Chaz, make a note to look into the turnover of Rising Sun's freighter crews."

"Thank you for coming to our assistance. We are a planet with a small population and are nearly defenseless against the likes of Rising Sun Industries. They will eventually wear us down. Losing the advisorship is a huge blow. If you can find them, if they are still alive, I would be forever in your debt."

"Our ship is already scanning the entire area where they could be. We'll talk to some people, too. It's important for us to find them as well, and it's refreshing to meet someone who is opposed to Frenzik and his Rising Sun Industries. Too many welcome him and hand him the keys to their planet."

"What does he do with them? How can one person control a dozen planets?" the Supreme Leader wondered.

"I can only speculate based on what he's done so far. He is trying to turn the populations into unwitting slaves. The planets of the Barrier Nebula are only a first step. Once he's solidified his control here, I think he'll move deeper into the Federation. I fear that he'll start a war. I don't want that, and neither do any of the cultured planets."

"The Albions seem to want that. Why are they so big? They are insufferable giants."

"That's why they're insufferable. They use their size to intimidate others. Good thing that doesn't work on us. Pound for pound, they're not as good at fighting as my people." Rivka bowed her head. "We'll leave you to it. We have to go because there are other planets that need our help fighting off Rising Sun's encroachment. We need to educate them before they invite Frenzik to take them over.

"It's not illegal to hand over your governments to private corporations. The Federation doesn't get involved in the internal affairs of planets except when it affects the Federation. Change of leadership does not change being a signatory of the Federation Charter."

The Supreme Leader dipped his head to Rivka.

Effir met Rivka and her team outside the office. "We have a banquet in your honor," she reiterated.

Rivka had forgotten. She was ready to return to the ship, but the *Wyatt Earp* was no longer at the spaceport. She'd have them pick her and the team up since she didn't want to squeeze into the bus another time.

"A banquet sounds wondrous. Lead on."

CHAPTER ELEVEN

Wyatt Earp, Government Building, Center of Town
Red stared at Rivka, daring her to make eye contact. Small people ate small foods in small quantities. The banquet was enough for a single plate for any one member of Rivka's crew, given their juiced metabolisms and size.

Rivka wouldn't look at him, just waved him and Lindy away. Rivka and Sahved stepped close to the table to take a single bite-sized piece of some sauteed vegetable.

"This is great. Thank you for hosting us." Rivka was genuinely pleased by the society that recognized Frenzik for what he was and for giving her the respect she'd earned by fighting for the rights of the good people in the Federation.

Magistrate, Frenzik has appeared over Albion, Clevarious reported.

Rivka held a finger to her ear and thought for a moment, then approached the Supreme Leader. "We have to go. A suspect has been spotted. They've been elusive and will disappear quickly. It's imperative that we go after them now."

The Supreme Leader summoned Effir. "Have the vehicle ready to go."

Rivka interrupted, "If it's okay, we'll have my ship pick us up right out front of this building. We need to go quickly."

Effir looked up at Rivka. "I understand that your team was extremely uncomfortable on the ride in. We apologize. Our vehicles are not large enough for human-sized guests."

"We apologize for being human-sized." Rivka laughed. "You are far too kind. We need to spend more time with the Efrahimi. You are delightful."

"We've heard that we are boring," the Supreme Leader replied.

"We'll continue searching for signs of the advisorship. We'll leave no stone unturned, no avenue of inquiry unexplored," Rivka promised.

Effir opened the door. Red went into the hallway first. The rest of the group followed. They walked as fast as Effir could go.

Right out front. Make sure you're visible so it doesn't spook our hosts, Rivka told Clodagh.

The ship was waiting for them when they rushed through the side door, avoiding the rotating door. Ankh skipped past the door he was comfortable using to stay with the group.

The cargo ramp was open, and they entered that way instead of using the airlock. Time was of the essence.

Cole hammered the button to close the ramp as the ship veered skyward. The instant the cargo hatch was secured, the Gate formed, and *Wyatt Earp* slipped through to materialize in orbit over Albion. Frenzik's ship *Rising Sun* was right in front of them.

"Frenzik," Rivka said when she walked onto the bridge.

"Your appearances are getting annoying," Frenzik replied.

"Heave to," Rivka ordered. She drew her finger across her throat. "Hit him with the EMP weapon."

"Five seconds," Clodagh announced.

Rivka counted down.

"Energy spiking, but it's too late," Clevarious said.

"Firing," Clodagh said and pointed at the main screen. Unlike normal weapons, there was nothing to see.

"Did it work?" Rivka asked.

"Energy is spiking."

"See where he goes," Rivka said, her voice louder and angrier than she wanted it to be. The ship jerked sideways to get a better view through the Gate. "It's not surprising that his systems are protected against an EMP."

Rising Sun raced through the Gate and was gone.

"Tell me you saw where he went," Rivka asked.

"We are correlating the view with our star charts," Clevarious said. "We will figure out where he's going."

Rivka expected an answer in seconds. After a minute, her patience ran out. "C?"

"We believe the location might be beyond the nebula, where our star charts are imprecise."

"See if you can access exploration data in any of the servers of the twelve planets. What about Tree? Can he find something?"

"Tree is occupied by integrating and unavailable at the moment," Clevarious replied.

Rivka paced. "We saw where he went, and we still don't know where he is," she grumbled. "No wonder he goes there."

"My thoughts exactly," Clodagh agreed. "Is there distortion within the nebula itself which would make it difficult to match up a location?"

"Excellent point. Adjusting for distortion," Clevarious said. "And there we are. It's only five light-years away. There's an exoplanet just within the nebula."

"No wonder he goes there," Rivka replied. "Take us to him. Prepare the railgun. If he doesn't want to play nice, neither will we."

"Spinning up the Gate drive," Clevarious reported.

Rivka took the captain's seat, steepled her fingers, and rested her chin on them.

Wyatt Earp accelerated over the event horizon and into the nebula.

"Frenzik, heave to or be fired upon."

A new voice replied. "Mister Frenzik isn't here. Can I take a message?"

"Heave to. If we see your Gate drive energize, I will fire. I'm done playing games with you. *Rising Sun* will be impounded, pending resolution on the question of use of restricted Federation technology. Impoundment is a much better option than being destroyed."

Rivka pointed at the screen.

"Prepare to fire."

"Gate drive is powering down," Clevarious said.

"Cole, get your team in their suits. On my command,

board and secure *Rising Sun*. Be prepared for your boarding to be opposed by a hostile crew."

"Roger," Cole confirmed.

Rivka looked at Clodagh. "Release *Destiny's Vengeance* and tether us to *Rising Sun*."

The voice returned. "We'll allow you to board us, but Mister Frenzik is not here."

"It's the technology you shouldn't have that interests us. That's what the warrant is for. Nothing personal about Malpace Frenzik. Please do not make any hostile moves against the boarding team. Follow their directions, and no one will be harmed."

Rivka gestured to close the channel.

She snarled. "Where's Frenzik?"

"Isn't that the million-credit question?" Clodagh asked. She shared a look with Rivka, confused and concerned.

"He's stirring up trouble while leading us on a wild bistok chase. I'm angry, but more at me than anyone else. Of course he pulled us around the nebula, chasing after him. Does he have a second ship with Gate technology?"

"We'd see it if it showed up at any of the twelve planets. Our drones will detect ships coming through the system Gate or using a Gate drive. No, he's not coming in behind us, so what is he doing?" Clodagh asked.

"Instead of leading us around the Barrier Nebula, he's taking care of business. Sending his boys to Finx to take over. I will speculate that he's kidnapping or murdering those who stand in his way. Innocent until proven guilty, but I'm following leads, and his name comes up an awful lot for there not to be a connection. I don't believe in coincidences, and I know that sometimes there's smoke without fire. That's why we investigate."

"That's why you grab them and shake the truth out of them," Clodagh added.

"There is that." Rivka chuckled. When she looked up, she wore her game face—the look that had convicted dozens. "Clevarious, get into the computer on that ship. I want to know everything there is to know about their Gate drive, where that ship's been, and where Frenzik is right now."

"I may have to employ greater assets to accomplish such a task."

"Beg Erasmus on my behalf. Does the boarding team have one of Ankh's coins?"

"They will momentarily. I'll have one delivered to them for installation on the bridge of *Rising Sun*." Ankh's coin was a hacking tool the Crenellian had developed that had given him covert access to hundreds of systems without having to get creative with hacking. When put in close proximity to a computer system, it created a physical bridge over which Ankh and Erasmus had complete access to the computer. They had rooted out files and information many times to confirm that someone was lying or hiding the truth.

The data didn't lie, according to the Singularity.

Rivka wanted more information that she didn't have to rip from a suspect's mind.

"This is Cole. Cargo ramp is open, and the squad is ready to deploy. We'll have to go two by two through the airlock. It's not very large. Furny and I first, then Lewis and Russell. Underway." The link remained open, and they could hear him breathing slowly and steadily. A clunk sounded when he contacted the manual override. He cranked it open and climbed inside.

In the airlock, the powered systems were operational. A push of a button pressurized the space until it equalized with the interior of the ship.

"Going in," Cole reported.

Cole kept his helmet on. The powered combat suit projected details he couldn't sense on his heads-up display, like infrared, ultraviolet, millimeter wave, and enhanced audio pickup. Cole transmitted the data to *Wyatt Earp*.

The corridor outside the airlock was empty, but the infrared sensors showed bodies in doorways and hatches lining the corridor and at the junctions.

"Looks like they aren't very neighborly," Cole said. "Securing the corridor until Russell and Lewis make it inside."

Cole went to the right, and Furny went left. They stopped and blocked the corridor, weapons raised, then waited. It took a minute and a half for the other two warriors to clear the airlock. Cole and Lewis continued down the corridor.

"Stand down. Step back from the corner, or you risk being injured," Cole warned the group ahead.

An Albion reached around the corner and fired an electronic weapon, some kind of stunner. Two probes shot from it and attached to the combat suit. The wires sparked and crackled.

When Cole brushed the wires away, the shooter looked perplexed. Cole surged forward, and after a single punch to the chest, the Albion slammed off the far bulkhead and crumpled to the deck. Cole raised his oversized railgun. "If I fire this thing, it's going to punch a lot of small holes in the hull. I'm protected from space, but what about you? Attack me again, and you seal your fate."

The belligerent crew hunched their shoulders and stood in defeat.

"Sit your asses down. I don't need you trying to loom over me." Cole turned up the volume on his external speakers to make his voice boom and echo. Even in armor, he was shorter than the Albions, but thanks to a ship built to accommodate them, he could easily fit through the corridors and hatches.

The other warriors watched them on IR to make sure they didn't bunch up or move about the ship.

Cole knew where the bridge was. They had scanned *Rising Sun* in their numerous engagements. It was centrally located—a survivability building technique for warships since, given the external sensors and systems, no one needed to look through transparent aluminum to see where they were going.

Cole headed toward the auxiliary stairs, avoiding the numerous elevators scattered throughout the ship. Before he reached the steps, the artificial gravity was turned off. He activated his boots and attached them to the deck, then detached and stepped through the hatch. He opted to use his pneumatic jets to expedite the short trip.

He settled to the deck, reviewed the HUD to make sure the data was up to the second, and moved into a corridor with a straight shot to the bridge. "Turn on the gravity!" Cole boomed.

He took three more steps before the artificial gravity returned.

"Thank you." He thought he would throw them a bone for complying. He could also use his railgun more easily in the center of the ship if they realized being without gravity only hampered their efforts and not his, but he didn't want them thinking that fighting back was a viable option. He readied his weapon. The bridge hatch was secured. "Nice try."

He stepped back, took aim, and peppered the hatch and surrounding bulkhead with five seconds of automatic fire from his oversized railgun. He slung the railgun and used the full power of his suit to twist the central wheel, which squealed in protest but turned. When the door popped free, Cole ripped it open, attempting to tear it off its hinges.

Inside, the crew was destroying equipment.

"Stop," Cole ordered mildly while raising his railgun.

They didn't. He obliged them by raking the space with his railgun. When he let go of the trigger, no one moved. He carefully stepped onto the bridge and placed Ankh's coin under the remains of what he thought was the main computer bank.

The destruction was limited to smashed screens.

"This is Cole," he transmitted to *Wyatt Earp*. "Coin is in place. They destroyed their monitors and interfaces, but I think the computers are operational. I interrupted them. Made it through the hatch quicker than they expected, I guess. Sucks to be them. None survived on the bridge."

"Thanks, Cole," Rivka replied. "We're going to come alongside and link up the airlocks. I'll be over shortly. Secure the crew. They may become prisoners, or they might not. That's up to what we find in those computers if they've left anything for us. I hope they did because I have lots of questions, and we can't be dithering around because Frenzik is somewhere other than here, wreaking havoc. I shudder to think!"

CHAPTER TWELVE

***Wyatt Earp* and *Rising Sun*, Barrier Nebula**
Rivka strolled through the airlock into *Rising Sun*. It was the first Albion ship she'd been on, and the first thing that struck her was its size. Cole hadn't mentioned how easy it was for them to get around. It was refreshing after riding on the Efrahimi bus.

The warriors had moved the crew to three separate places inside the ship. There were no others on board unless they could defeat IR and *Wyatt Earp's* more intense sensor systems.

Red stayed by Rivka's side, with Lindy right behind her. The bodyguards were fully armed and covered in ballistic protection. Rivka only wore the vest.

With the bridge crew gone, who do you recommend we talk with first? Rivka asked.

Cole replied, *The group closest to you. I don't know who's important on this ship. They're all full of bluster and bullshit. Typical Albions.*

"Now, now," Rivka said out loud. Cole wouldn't hear.

He was on the bridge doing what Erasmus told him to do. "Not all Albions are jagoffs, are they?"

"It's bad to generalize," Lindy agreed.

"But we have yet to meet one who wasn't. I fear they're living down to the bad stereotype they've established."

"It's well deserved," Red mumbled. "Limp dicks."

"Don't get in their faces, Red. Let me talk with them while they're not riled up." Rivka headed to the mess deck, where the warriors had sequestered the biggest group. When she arrived, she found many of the Albions sporting bruises or putting pressure on cuts.

"Furny?" Rivka asked.

"They thought they could storm their way past me. Poor decision-making on their part, followed by poor execution. To their credit, they learned fast. They're much more docile now." Furny stood like a monument to war in the combat suit with his weapon trained on the subdued detainees.

Rivka had every intention of letting them go, but they weren't playing to her better nature.

"Everyone sit where you are. I'll walk around and talk with each of you individually."

She reached the first Albion, a female. "Where's Frenzik?" she asked with her hand on the detainee's shoulder. Her mind showed where they'd last seen him: leaving on a shuttle while they were in orbit over Albion.

She asked the next Albion a different question to keep them guessing.

"What are you doing in this part of space?"

The Albion had no idea. He didn't have anything to do with where they went or what they did. He was confused.

"Why is *Rising Sun* taking over other planets?"

An older female Albion had it clear in her mind. Domination. The Albions were the species to rule the rest. She resented humanity's penetration into the sector and the Federation's restrictive and nonsensical rules. She had nothing but hatred for Rivka.

"Finally, someone who's honest," the Magistrate noted.

"I didn't say a word. If being present is being honest, then we are all honest," the female suggested.

"As you wish," Rivka replied, then moved on to the next and the next. The younger crew members knew nothing. They were the working staff of the ship. The older crew? They were the Rising Sun Industries insiders, but the clarity of their thoughts wasn't what Rivka had wished for.

Frenzik hadn't shared where he was going with any of them. The bridge crew had been killed, so they weren't available to answer her questions.

"Next group." She stood on shaky legs. Red caught her and dipped an arm under hers and around her shoulders.

"This was the biggest group. There are fewer Albions in the next group and just a handful in the last group," Red told her.

"I'll be fine," Rivka replied. She straightened, took a deep breath, and walked through the hatch. She headed down one level and into the corridor that led to where the next group was sequestered. There were only eight, a low number for which she was grateful. "Line 'em up, and I'll knock 'em down."

"Sit there and don't be annoying, or you'll find yourselves on the wrong end of my fist," Red announced.

"I guess that's one way to do it," Rivka whispered to Lindy.

Lindy just shook her head.

The fluttering of wings alarmed them all.

"If you'll excuse me." Lindy darted from the space to intercept Dery in the corridor. "You shouldn't be here."

The answer is not here, the boy told them. *Twin stars will shine the light.*

Rivka joined Lindy and Dery in the corridor. She held out her arm and he landed, then held onto Rivka's head to steady himself.

"You're saying we're wasting our time. I'm inclined to believe you." He leaned his forehead toward her, and she responded in kind until their foreheads touched. Peace and calm washed over her. "Thanks, little man."

Rivka paused while Red moved through the hatch. Lewis waited inside with the detainees.

"Magistrate?" Red wondered.

Clevarious, are any of the planets of the Barrier Nebula in a system with two stars? Rivka requested.

That would be Glazoron, Clevarious replied.

Rivka twirled her finger. "That's it. Return to *Wyatt Earp*. It's time to leave." She didn't say their destination out loud, not that the crew of *Rising Sun* could do anything about it. "Did Cole get that Gate drive removed yet?"

Lewis relayed the question. "He and Clodagh are almost finished."

"Watch this mob until our people are back on the ship, then retrograde. Button it up on your way out and leave them to it." Rivka leaned into the space and spoke to the detainees. "We'll put out an emergency call for a disabled ship. Since your crew tried to destroy your control systems, I have no obligation to fix your ship, so I'll leave you to it. Without a Gate drive, it could be a while before anyone gets to you."

Lindy recoiled. "You're going to abandon them?"

Rivka shook her head. "No. That would be condemning them all to death, and I can't do that. We'll drag them behind us through our Gate and dump them at the far reaches of the Albion system before we continue on."

Erasmus will fly Destiny's Vengeance *in tandem with us. We'll retether the ambassadors' ship after we've released* Rising Sun, Clevarious advised.

Rivka twirled her finger again, a gesture she'd learned from Terry Henry Walton. She was glad to use it.

"I'll carry you," Rivka told Dery. They strolled casually to the ladder and climbed up toward the airlock level. "You are a great help, as always, Dery, and thank you for the clarity."

The river flows inexorably toward the sea, the boy replied. He carried the knowledge of the faeries, which gave him a vocabulary that far exceeded that of most adults.

"I know. Our destiny lies ahead, not behind us." They continued through the airlock onto *Wyatt Earp*.

Red remained at the airlock to make sure only *Wyatt Earp's* crew transferred from *Rising Sun*.

Lindy took Dery from the Magistrate. *Smart people. Good people,* the boy said as they parted.

Rivka went straight to the bridge. She expected to see Clodagh since she always expected to see her chief engineer, although she knew Clodagh was on *Rising Sun* dismantling their Gate drive.

Aurora was there.

"Russell is just fine. Keeping the Albion crew on their butts while we extract what we can from their computers and help ourselves to their Gate drive. If we determine they developed it independently, then they can have it back, although it may not be completely operational when they get it."

Aurora nodded and smiled. "Thank you, Magistrate. I wasn't worried. He's tough, and in his combat armor, he's invincible."

"I sure hope so because if something happens to him, we only have three warriors, and we spent so much time bringing him up to speed. It would suck trying to replace him," Rivka deadpanned.

Aurora's mouth fell open.

Rivka laughed. "It would suck so bad."

"You're being mean," Aurora replied with a sly grin. "But I get your point. He's not invincible, and he better act like it!"

Rivka tapped her nose.

The clump-clump of heavy tread echoed down the corridor. Clodagh appeared outside the bridge. "The Albion's Gate drive is going to Engineering, where we can take a good look at it."

"Or we could take it to R2D2 and let them dissect it," Rivka suggested.

"Ankh and Erasmus requested first dibs."

"They said 'first dibs?'"

"I'm paraphrasing," Clodagh clarified. "They also were able to download the complete database from the ship's computers. It seems the crew didn't destroy anything important. Replace the monitors and interfaces, and the ship will be back in business, all except for the ability to form their own Gates."

Cole strode down the passage, around the corner by the bridge, and to the cargo hold to clean and store his gear. Furny, Lewis, and Russell appeared. Red took care of the airlock.

"All secure," he shouted down the corridor.

"Aurora, tether that ship and take us to the farthest limit of the Albion gravity well."

The pilot input the data while Clevarious made the calculations. A Gate appeared next to them, and *Destiny's Vengeance* slipped through. *Wyatt Earp's* Gate appeared a moment later. The ship accelerated over the event horizon to appear in the darkness of Albion space. They were so far from the star that it appeared little larger than the surrounding starfield.

"Send out a distress call with coordinates."

"Sent," Clevarious replied instantly.

"Tether *Destiny's Vengeance* and take us to Glazoron. Shoot for a high orbit so we can see what kind of ships are there. Wait to request clearance to land until we get a better picture, like where Frenzik might be."

"Consider it done." Aurora tapped a final key and leaned back. They headed through the Gate into Glazoron's space.

"Sahved!" Rivka yelled over her shoulder. "Brief me on Glazoron while the rest of these good people conduct a little technical surveillance."

Rivka stood and motioned for Clodagh to take the captain's chair.

Clodagh pointed in the other direction. "I was going to go play with the Albion Gate drive. I mean, help take it apart."

Rivka pursed her lips but ended with a nod and returned to the captain's seat. "Send Sahved here instead of the conference room, please."

"Will do. Thanks, Magistrate."

"Hey, babe," Lewis said from the corridor.

"Get in here, you stowaway reprobate." Rivka rotated the chair until she faced the warrior. "You're Aurora's boyfriend."

"Magistrate!" the pilot called in an exasperated tone.

"I feel like I did something wrong. My ass-chewings usually come from Cole. Maybe I'm moving up in the world."

"You know what they say, Russell. Everyone likes a little ass. No one likes a smart ass." Rivka winked at him, then pointed over her shoulder with her thumb. "Why does she think you're invincible in your combat armor?"

Russell nodded and smiled. "I may have implied that the suits are indestructible. That's on me."

Rivka turned serious. "You know that Ramses was killed while wearing his armor. Cory was crushed for years. Don't do that to my pilot. Sure, she'll find another guy, probably better than you, but she'd be a little upset until a new guy comes along."

"I'll do my best to not let you down, Magistrate. I know very well about Ramses. All four of us were on Benitus Seven. The Skrima came straight from the deepest pits of hell. I don't ever want to relive that engagement."

"I don't blame you. You're not invincible. If you die, I'll kill you myself," Rivka promised.

"What?" Russell was confused.

"Aurora, take ten. We're not going anywhere for a little bit. Go convince your boyfriend to be, I don't know, less of a nob and more of an upfront, straight-up kind of guy."

"I don't know what that means, but an ass-kicking is in order," Aurora promised.

Sahved hovered outside the bridge.

The pilot and her boyfriend raced down the corridor.

"Did I interrupt?" Sahved apologized.

"Not at all. I was performing my relationship management duties as *Wyatt Earp's* matriarch."

"You are?" Sahved ducked his head to enter the bridge.

"Who else would it be?"

"Are we required to have a mother? Mine is back on Yemilore. I'm good. If I want to be yelled at for being a third deputy undersecretary and not someone of import, then I will call her for my appropriate comeuppance."

Rivka snorted and chuckled. "I guess that's it exactly. These guys don't have their mothers. I don't really want to be their mother as I'm too young for that. I would expect my children to be much younger and, of course, better behaved, like Dery. He's a good boy."

"Dery is the faeries' savior. You can't compare him to anyone else. Not a normal human, anyway," Sahved replied stoically. "He is the most faerie of any faerie. The faeriest of all faeries."

"I'm not sure that sounds like you expect. Where were we? Glazoron. You've got four minutes to get me up to speed."

CHAPTER THIRTEEN

Wyatt Earp, in Orbit above Glazoron

Sahved twirled his fingers, then clasped his hands before him and leaned forward.

"Four minutes. Okay." He took a deep breath. "Glazoron has two stars and orbits in a figure eight with temperature extremes. The people on the planet are extremely hardy. They are humanoid but grow hair that becomes fur when they loop far beyond, then shed all of it to be nearly bald for the close pass. They are unique in the Federation in their evolution. They are about the height of a human but have a layer of fat that aids in the growth and later repulsion of hair, so they tend to look roundish.

"From a cultural perspective, they are hierarchical, much like Yemilore. We have tiers. Work your way up the chain or down, but you're always on the move. Otherwise, you're stagnant and destined for the most complete of abject failures."

"Who's the person in charge, and more to the point of

Rising Sun Industries, what happened to their leadership council or whatever that prompted the notification to the High Chancellor?" Rivka wondered.

"Nine, three, one. Nine medium ministers who report to three high ministers who report to his Preeminent Supremeness."

"Is that his title? I'm going to meet with the Preeminent Supremeness?"

"And he's a round one. Hairy when the occasion warrants and billiard-ball hairless at other times. The high ministers are missing. They went home one night and never returned. Their spouses swear they never arrived home."

"More alien abductions. Were there bistok mutilations to go along with the disappearances?" Rivka asked.

"I don't think so, but I'll review the reports and dig deeper. I'm sorry for my failure. I am completely dressed down. You *are* the matriarch!"

"You're not dressed down. I was kidding, so don't be freaky. Any leads on where Frenzik might be?"

Sahved brightened immediately. "I am so very freaky! No leads on Frenzik, but the industry he is taking over here is textiles and high-tech manufacture. They have sheepik and alpacalacas, which both grow the most robust and desired coats. Their coats become our coats."

"Textiles? Who cares about that when they have high-tech manufacture that can produce Gate drives if they have the raw materials, the likes of which they could get from Hergin?" Rivka rolled her eyes. "Frenzik is leading us on a wild goose chase, but Dery was convinced our answer was here, so we'll stay here until we get to the bottom of it. We'll even freeze traffic out of Glazoron if needed. We're going to find Frenzik, and I'm going to interrogate him. I'll find what he's hiding."

"We look forward to that revelation," Sahved replied.

Rivka spun her chair to focus on the main screen. Data scrolled, and the tactical view remained populated with a sparse mix of freighters and shuttles.

"Warships," Aurora stated, pointing at the main screen.

A group of four ships appeared from behind a planet mid-system.

"Does Glazoron have their own space fleet?"

"They do not," Clevarious confirmed.

"Bring the gravitic shields online, and recall Clodagh and Aurora to the bridge. Fire up the ion cannon. We'll see if a few shots across their bows convince them to steer clear of this fight. Before we fire, analyze those ships. Do they have enough firepower to cause us any problems?"

Clevarious replied. "They have scattering technology employed, so our scans are inconclusive."

"We can't see shit besides that they're big, armed, and not freighters," Rivka suggested.

"They look like two cruisers, a destroyer, and a frigate. There also appear to be drones or space fighters that have sallied forth from them. Maybe one of the cruisers is a carrier. We'll get more clarity once we close the distance."

Clodagh ran onto the bridge. "Who wants to start a war?" she asked after a brief examination of the main screen. "I'll take Weapons Control."

She moved to a station that was usually vacant and

surrounded herself with the cutting-edge technology *Wyatt Earp* employed. It was Ankh's weapons testbed, part of his work with Ted and R2D2, the Federation's elite research and development branch.

Rivka accessed the intercom. "All hands, prepare for combat. Cole, get your people in their suits. We have four unidentified warships bearing down on us. We're not going to tolerate that. I'll keep you informed as the situation unfolds."

"Woohoo!" Red shouted from down the corridor. "We need a door gun that I can mount!"

Clodagh stopped what she was doing and turned to Rivka. They made faces at each other.

"We do not need you humping a big gun," Rivka called over her shoulder. "Give me a broadcast channel targeted at those ships."

"Broad beam is live," Clodagh said. She worked two stations at the same time, fingers flying as she moved back and forth. The main screen populated with the weapon systems' availability. Everything was green, including missiles Rivka didn't remember having. *Destiny's Vengeance* showed up as a separate system with its weapons coming online. The tether had been released, and Ankh's ship had moved abeam *Wyatt Earp*.

"Inbound ships to Glazoron. This is Magistrate Rivka Anoa in the heavy frigate *Wyatt Earp*. I am here on behalf of the Federation in the conduct of an ongoing investigation of criminal activity in the Barrier Nebula. We request you identify yourselves and your intentions."

"Do you think they'll answer?" Clodagh wondered.

The comm system automatically repeated the message three times.

"I'm starting to think they won't," Rivka replied. She steepled her fingers and watched the two formations approach each other on the tactical display.

"They'll be in estimated weapons range in less than a minute," Clodagh reported.

"We'll stay within weapons range for thirty seconds. We'll fire a few shots across their bow. If they don't fire at us, we'll loop back to remain between them and the planet. Same with *Destiny's Vengeance*. We'll split up if we need to attack. Take out the cruiser and the carrier first."

"What about the drones or space fighters, whatever they are?" Clodagh asked.

"Hit them with the EMP weapon. They can float dead in space until someone comes and picks them up. They'll have their environmental protection suits on, so they'll be better protected, rather than hit the bigger ships with it."

"In weapons range," Clodagh stated in a cold, hard voice.

"That means they're in range of *our* weapons. Energize the EMP. Prepare to disable those small ships or drones or whatever the hell they are. Prepare to fire the ion cannon." Rivka waited. The small armada continued flying toward *Wyatt Earp*, adjusting course as the Magistrate's ship moved away from the planet. "It's confirmed. They're coming for us. Fire the EMP."

There were no signs that the weapon had fired besides a small gauge on the weapons board turning from green to red.

"Fire the cannon. Three shots angled across the front of their formation."

"Seventy percent of the small ships have been disabled. The remainder have pulled off-course and are evading and heading away from their formation," Clevarious announced.

The four ships opened fire, sending a stream of high-velocity projectiles and plasma in *Wyatt Earp's* direction. Nose-on approach gave the enemy little in the way of an aiming point, but the volume of fire filled the space within which *Wyatt Earp* flew.

They were close enough that the incoming arrived quickly. The ship bumped and swayed with the dispersion of energy as it was redirected past the hull.

"Shields are intact. No damage." Clodagh pumped her fist and prepared new targets, no longer aiming across their bows.

"Well, now. Wasn't that delightful?" Rivka asked. More incoming splashed across the shields. "Fire the cannon. Two shots at the cruiser, two at the carrier. Then Gate us to a position behind them."

"Firing," Clodagh said.

"Gate is forming." Aurora continued forward at a steady speed, and the ship entered the Gate and reappeared behind the enemy formation. *Destiny's Vengeance* materialized on their flank and delivered withering fire into the closest ship, sending its reactor critical. When the frigate exploded, it released the blinding light of a nuclear blast.

The remaining three ships veered away from the explosion, and a voice sounded over the comm channel. "Cease fire, cease fire! Whoever is shooting at us, stop what you're doing."

"Hold your fire," Rivka said loud enough to be heard on the open channel. "Deploying your fighters and approaching us comms silent, then firing on us, was a poor decision on your part. Stand down. Bring your ships to a full stop and prepare to be boarded."

"You showed up out of nowhere in an abnormal orbit. What were we supposed to think?"

"You were supposed to answer my hail. But let's not look back at your cascade of failures that resulted in the complete destruction of one of your ships and the disabling of seventy percent of your fighters. Also, it appears the minimal fire we delivered on your two larger vessels has caused some damage. I'm sorry you thought you could intimidate me."

"I don't see you stopping. When I close this channel, I will destroy your entire fleet. I've already declared you enemies of the Federation. At this point, you are nothing more than criminals looking for a way out of the mess that you created."

"Enemy ships are slowing." Clodagh sounded disappointed. "Are we going to board them?"

"No. I'm not boarding an enemy cruiser. There are way too many of them, and they're geared for battle. It wouldn't turn out well for us, no matter how invincible Russell thinks he is." Rivka unmuted her microphone. "Enemy ship, who are you, and what are you doing here?"

"My name is Dagmar of the Private Merchant Fleet. We patrol all twelve populated planets of the Barrier Nebula."

Rivka wasn't convinced. "Please define what you mean by 'patrol.'"

"We ensure the safety and security of all shipping in these systems."

"By attacking me, you ensured my safety. I feel we have different definitions of the word 'safety.' Who do you work for?"

"We're a private consortium," Dagmar answered.

"That's nice. You're telling me that you're independently wealthy, and these planets resupply you out of the kindness of their hearts. I'll save us both the time by telling you what you are. You're a pirate fleet in the employ of Rising Sun Industries, specifically Malpace Frenzik. You create fear so that he can dig his hooks even deeper into these planets. Guarantor of peace and stability when he is the sole creator of the instability."

Rivka jabbed a finger at the main screen. A small parade of ships was headed away from Glazoron. "Shut down the system Gate before anyone can use it. We'll talk to each of those ships to see if our Mister Frenzik is trying to escape. Wouldn't that be nice of him, to hand himself over like that?"

"I'll take care of it," Clevarious said.

"Where were we?" Rivka started afresh. "That's right. We're talking about your duplicity in creating the crises you alone can solve. Those used to be called protection rackets. People paid for you not to harass them. It's quite illegal, I'll have you know. Looks like I'm going to have to impound your ships before they are dismantled and sold for scrap."

"You can't do that!" Dagmar blurted. "We're a private company."

"With big weapons that you shouldn't have."

The carrier eased in front of the cruiser, and the destroyer lined up close behind.

"Energy is spiking. A Gate is forming."

"Fire," Rivka ordered. "On the cruiser."

The ships shot toward the Gate like launched rockets but a pulse from *Wyatt Earp* disrupted its formation. It fizzled. The fighters that had survived the EMP continued on their trajectories.

"All ships in the Glazoron system, you are ordered to land at the spaceport on the planet, where you will submit to questioning by the Magistrate. Any deviation from these orders will be dealt with harshly."

Clodagh stated, "By 'harshly,' you mean they will be destroyed."

"It's not like they're leaving us a choice. Those on the planet are the innocents, but those in space surrounding Glazoron are suspects in an investigation that now includes maintaining a pirate fleet to extort credits and favors from the legitimate governments. The only question I have is why we haven't seen or heard of this clown show before now."

Clevarious answered, "Despite the time we've spent in the Barrier Nebula, we've had very little interaction with the locals. Those who would inform us of the issues plaguing their planets have disappeared, and you can't read their minds like you can your fellow humans."

"Humans are easy," Rivka replied. "These races are hard. I found that out on *Rising Sun*. Getting into their minds was challenging. Painful, even. I'm still suffering from the effects." Rivka rubbed her temple. "I think that's why I have no patience with these people. We'll see what we can get from them when they're on the ground."

She nodded at Aurora. "Follow them in. We'll be the last to land. Let's keep *Destiny's Vengeance* in orbit should anyone sneak around us."

CHAPTER FOURTEEN

***Wyatt Earp*, Landing Pad 69, Glazoron Conclave**
Rivka strolled off the ship in Red's shadow. He was covered from neck to toe in ballistic armor. His helmet was fastened tightly to remain in place while he scanned the extensive parking lot filled with ships of all shapes and sizes. The Private Merchant Fleet's cruisers and carrier were immense compared to every other ship at the spaceport, easily ten times the size of *Wyatt Earp*. Up close, the two were easily distinguishable. The cruiser was heavily armed, while the carrier had bay after bay lining the sides.

The Magistrate had allowed the carrier to recover their surviving fighters, all of which were unmanned, they later discovered. Had she known, she wouldn't have been so accommodating.

In powered combat armor, Cole and his team flanked Rivka and Red. Sahved and Lindy followed.

"We've ordered the crews to meet us on the tarmac," Rivka said. "We'll see if they comply. Clevarious is scanning the ships to see if anyone remains on board."

Red focused on the nearest cruiser. "Son of a mother fuck." He tipped his chin toward the ship. "Albions."

"No wonder they thought they could intimidate us. It's their way." Rivka shrugged. "Remember, no generalizing."

"They live down to it." Red hefted his railgun. "Pretty much every single one we've met so far, but maybe the nice ones don't come out during the daytime because the chaotic evil bastards ply the sunlight."

Red glanced at Rivka. "I think it's probably all of them. At least the ones in charge. Maybe we should find some Albion females and put them into the big chairs."

"The only chairs they have are big," Red muttered. "At least from my perspective. By the way, didn't you question some of their women on board *Rising Sun?*"

"They were different. All of them were Frenzik insiders, cut from the same cloth while also being different enough. I hope they were different." Rivka shook her head. The thought of looking into more Albion minds depressed her, but she had to do it.

Life sometimes led down a path from which there were no side trails. It was a river flowing to the sea.

Red powered ahead, staying slightly in front of the Magistrate. Lindy stayed close to her. They unconsciously fell into sync with the warriors' mechanized footsteps.

They went across the landing field to the Albion cruiser masquerading as a free trader. The Albion crew was standing outside. Cole and Furny jumped forward and ran straight at the crew. They staggered back under the perceived onslaught, and the two warriors ground to a halt. Cole delivered the order. "Sit your asses down!"

"I wonder where he learned that?" Red asked over his shoulder.

"You can't mean me. I would never say anything so untoward." Rivka wouldn't meet Red's glance. She brightened. With the warriors to cow Frenzik's mercenaries, Rivka's job would be easier. "Where's the captain?" she asked. "Which one of you is Dagmar?"

"I'm Dagmar," an older Albion said.

A second Albion stood and shouted, "I'm Dagmar," then a third and a fourth. Cole rushed over and shoved them back to the ground.

C, give me a voice analysis. Were any of those knuckleheads Dagmar?

Clevarious analyzed the voices that had been transmitted to the ship via the combat suits.

The first one, Magistrate.

Rivka walked up to him. "Dagmar. I'd say it was nice to meet you, but it's not." She didn't have far to lean to be even with his head. She put her hand on his shoulder. "Where's Frenzik?"

Instant panic. He wasn't expecting the question, although from Rivka's perspective, he should have been since she had focused on nothing else. He thought about the surface of Glazoron. Frenzik had taken a shuttle from space.

Rivka took a couple steps away. *C, lock down this planet. Frenzik is here somewhere.*

"He's not out here," Red added.

Rivka nodded and went to the next Albion before

reaching back. "How do you earn your credits?" she asked the captain.

Intercept freighters not flying the Rising Sun Industries flag.

"I think we've seen what we need to see," Rivka said. "Cole, head inside and dismantle that Gate drive."

"Wait a minute!" The captain jumped to his feet. Red punched him in the gut. When the captain doubled over, Red kicked his legs out from under him, and the Albion hit the tarmac hard.

"Your Gate drive is questionable technology and not intended for private use, and definitely not for use by pirates," Rivka explained. "And that is exactly what you are. You'll need to move clear of these three ships, as we're going to destroy them."

The captain composed himself enough to sit up. "All our personal belongings are on board. You have to let us remove our stuff."

Rivka didn't want to pay fair market value for their gear. Otherwise, it would have been an illegal taking.

"You are correct. We don't have time to escort your people in, so what we're going to do is destroy your weapons and the ability of this ship to fly. It'll be permanently grounded. Then you can take your stuff off at your leisure."

"Then what are we supposed to do?" The captain glared at Red.

"I recommend engaging in a legal line of work. As it is, what you were doing is illegal, and you should probably be in Jhiordaan. You and your fellow captains, at the very least. Unless you help us with our current investigation.

Then we could settle for the removal of your ships' operational capabilities. Red, take him into custody."

"My pleasure, Magistrate." Red yanked the captain to his feet but held his arm low so the prisoner had to walk hunched over.

"Lindy, Lewis, and Furny with me. We need to take two more captains into custody." It had been Rivka's plan to take the captains into custody all along. She wanted to give them a brief moment of hope that they wouldn't be arrested so they would be more pliable about providing information about who tasked them. It was Rising Sun Industries, but she needed them to say it was Frenzik. She needed their statements on record to give her more firepower to take him down.

The captains were obvious. Furny grabbed one, and Lewis seized the other. They frog-marched them across the tarmac toward *Wyatt Earp*, but the heavy frigate was no longer there.

Rivka stopped. "Did they cloak the ship?" She tried contacting them directly. *Clevarious? Open the cargo bay door so we can see where we're going. If I crush my face on an invisible ship, I'll be very put out.*

Lindy picked up a rock and tossed it. It sailed through the space where the ship had been and bounced on the tarmac. They watched it skip across the concrete and come to rest forty meters away.

"Cole, contact the ship, please. A 'by your leave' would have been nice, but they wouldn't have gone if they didn't have a reason. I hope they have Frenzik in their sights. That would rev my engine." Rivka waved at Cole to get to it.

He used his armored suit's comm, which was more robust than their comm chips. After a few moments, he explained, "They raced to the Gate. Looked like someone was making a run for it, and get this: they'd overridden the Gate lockout. It was active when they intercepted the ship. *Wyatt Earp* Gated from within the atmosphere. Otherwise, they would have never made it in time. They didn't have an opportunity to notify us."

"How did we miss the ship Gating out right over our heads?" Rivka wondered. "Never mind. We did, and they went for the right reason. I approve. What happened to *Destiny's Vengeance*? Do they have Frenzik?"

"It wasn't Frenzik. It was the three high ministers."

"Well, now! Things are looking up. I want to talk with them."

"They assumed. They're still dealing with the ship. They haven't quite boarded it yet," Cole said.

Rivka lost her smile. "Oh, no."

Cole nodded his helmeted head. "Tyler and Clodagh are the boarding party. *Destiny's Vengeance* is at the Gate, too. Ankh and Erasmus are studying why the high ministers were able to override the lockout."

"Do they have to board that ship?" Rivka closed her eyes and groaned. "Make sure there is no other way."

Cole passed the message and gave Rivka the thumbs-up.

Rivka didn't have a good feeling about it.

Wyatt Earp, Glazoron System Gate

Clodagh looked at Tyler and then through the airlock at

the ship on the other side. Random faces peered at her. "Are you sure?"

"There are only so many of us, and the job needs to be done," Tyler stated with the utmost confidence. "Plus, all we have are these axes. We're better without the railguns, don't you think?"

"There's one railgun in the locker."

Tyler froze. "Should we, you know, take it?"

"I don't want it. If we carry it, then we have to be ready to use it," Clodagh replied.

Tyler nodded. "We'll give it to Ryleigh or Kennedy to make sure no one tries to sneak through the airlock and onto *Wyatt Earp*."

"That's the most ridiculous thing I've ever heard. Can you imagine? One of our pilots with a railgun."

"They know how to shoot. Their boyfriends trained them."

"Ryleigh, get out here," Clodagh called to the bridge.

The young pilot appeared moments later. "You summoned the master of flight?" Ryleigh asked.

"Can you handle a railgun?" Tyler asked.

She laughed. "No." Ryleigh didn't explain further. She returned to the bridge.

"There's our answer," Clodagh stated.

"Clevarious, can you make sure no one sneaks onto *Wyatt Earp*?" Tyler asked.

"Of course," the SI replied. "But I can't be a deterrent. I suggest Aurora. She's the one who can handle the railgun."

"Why didn't I ask you in the first place?" Tyler wondered.

"I'm sure I don't know. Maybe next time."

Tyler nodded while flushing. "I'm embarrassed, C. Can you ask Aurora to come out here, please? I'll get the thunderstick."

He went to the weapons locker and retrieved Rivka's railgun. When he returned, he found Aurora waiting.

"Thanks for getting schooled up on this thing." He handed the weapon to her.

She checked it before slinging it under her arm. "You want me to shoot anyone who appears in the airlock?"

"Well, no. If that someone is us, we'd like to not be shot." Tyler studied her expression to see if she had been serious. She smiled and shrugged one shoulder. "You're not instilling me with a great deal of confidence."

"Are you sure you want to go over there?"

Tyler looked through the airlock at the round faces beyond. He didn't see any Albions, which was good. "No, I'm not sure I want to go, but I'm positive that we have to. We need to recover those three ministers so Rivka can talk with them. Maybe we can just ask whoever opens the airlock to send them over." Tyler looked hopeful.

"I'm all for that." She looked at the boarding axe in her hand. "Are we really going to carry these things?"

Tyler looked at his weapon for a moment before putting it down.

Clodagh placed hers against the bulkhead next to his. "Good call."

"You have to go with your strengths, right? How about we offer medical and engineering assistance for the ship?"

"I like that plan." She tipped her chin at the airlock. "They're waiting."

Tyler nodded once and headed in. At the far end, he

gestured for the Glazoron crew to open their outer hatch. He waited while the actuators cycled and the hatch popped open. An individual from inside the Glazoron ship pushed it open and stepped aside to reveal a crew member holding a hand blaster aimed into the airlock.

"Really?" Tyler leaned to the side so they could see Aurora holding the railgun. "If she fires that thing, it'll cut a hole right through your ship. Put your gun down, dumbass!"

The Glazoron holstered the pistol and stepped away.

Tyler didn't know what came over him. His heart skipped a beat to remind him that he wasn't in the direct action side of Rivka's business. He dealt with the consequences of those engagements.

"We can offer medical and engineering assistance," he said to the individual who had presented himself.

"I am Captain Glaziro-Rug. Why have you prevented us from leaving?"

Clodagh shook a finger at him. "You know very well that Magistrate Rivka Anoa is pursuing a suspect and has secured this system until Malpace Frenzik is in custody. Do you have any Albions on board?"

"We do not." He gestured broadly as if to say, "See for yourself."

"That's nice, but we'll settle for scanning your ship to find anyone who might be hiding, like our fugitive from justice, Mister Frenzik. We're also looking for the three high ministers. We'll need to bring them on board our ship for immediate transfer to Glazoron. The Magistrate would like to congratulate them on being found since they'd been reported missing, then discuss what happened. If you'll send them over, we'd appreciate it."

C, do you have their data on file so you can be sure it's them? Tyler asked.

I do. I'll ensure that anyone they send over is who we expect.

The captain stood in front of the hatch. He hadn't passed on any instructions and wasn't moving out of the way.

"How are your teeth? They seemed to be a shade crooked. I can straighten them for you if you'd like."

"My teeth?" The captain held his ground.

"If that's it, we'll disable your ship and leave you adrift so when Rivka is ready for you, we'll return. Until then, you can kiss my ass." Clodagh gave them the finger.

The captain returned the gesture and stepped aside.

C? Clodagh asked.

It's their greeting. You told him he was number one. He appreciates the recognition and deference and has afforded you the same courtesy.

"Really?" Tyler blurted. He whipped out his middle finger and thrust it in front of him.

They did the same.

He shook his head. "Can you send over the three high ministers, please?"

"Of course," the captain replied. He pointed, and three individuals tottered into view. They were dressed in robes versus the crew uniform like the others Tyler and Clodagh had seen.

"Please, step through and wait for us," Tyler ushered them toward Aurora, who wasn't amused by the double duty of guard and escort.

The three made it to *Wyatt Earp* and visibly relaxed when they got there.

"I'll put them in the conference room," Aurora said and followed them down the corridor, giving directions as they walked.

Clodagh stepped back to block the hatch to *Wyatt Earp*.

"I take it that you don't need any medical or engineering assistance, so with that, we'll be on our way as soon as we can be sure you cannot activate the Gate. I expect your computer systems have been taken over and scrubbed of the programming you used. Sorry about that, but fleeing a Magistrate's order is a crime. We'd like to prevent you from committing more crimes because no one wants to go to Jhiordaan."

We weren't able to get into their system. You're going to have to disable it manually, Clevarious told them.

Dammit! "On second thought," Tyler said aloud, "we'll have to see your bridge. Please, lead on." He waved for Clodagh to follow.

The one with the holstered pistol was tagged as their guide. Aurora hadn't returned yet, but Dery materialized in *Wyatt Earp's* outer hatch.

"You have to go back inside," Clodagh tried to herd the young boy in. He only giggled.

Whee! Floyd shouted and bounced over the coaming into the airlock.

We come too, Dery said.

The captain and the others looking through the hatch gawked. A murmur passed between them and they bowed, staying bent over and looking distinctly uncomfortable with their rounded bodies.

CHAPTER FIFTEEN

<u>Wyatt Earp</u> and the Glazoron Passenger Cruiser, near the System Gate

"You have their attention, Dery. Come on. If anyone finds out about this, I expect I'll be sent out the airlock in interstellar space," Tyler said. He walked in front of Dery, who flew casually through the airlock, waving at the Glazoron crew when he arrived. They remained bowed but looked out the sides of their eyes at him.

Tyler tapped their escort on the shoulder and gestured for him to lead the way.

"Haven't you ever seen a half-faerie before?"

"He is an archangel," the captain replied matter-of-factly. "I will escort you."

The one with the pistol bowed and backed away.

"Follow me, Your Grace," the captain said and hurried down the corridor.

"With me, little man." Tyler held out his arm for Dery to land and be carried. The boy wrapped his small arm around Tyler's neck while waving for Floyd to keep up with his free hand.

Tyler glanced back to find Clodagh and the rest of the Glazoron crew following. *Did you know they were going to react this way?*

It is bigger than me, Dery replied.

"Whatever that means, little man, I'm good with it. I like the wide corridors on this ship. It's nice to feel less constrained." Tyler looked around as if they were on a tour. He wasn't sure what they were going to do when they reached the bridge and hoped Clodagh knew. If not her, then Clevarious and the SI team from *Wyatt Earp.* If nothing else, he could ask Dery to order the Glazoron captain to delete the programming that had let them defeat the Gate's lockout.

Would he respond to such a request? Tyler hoped it wouldn't come to that since Dery, like the faeries on Azfelius, had his own agenda that went beyond human understanding.

But it was the purest of agendas. Dery only wanted peace. His ability to influence that had come in the Jack the Ripper case. The boy had saved them all.

It made Tyler feel guilty for calling one of the Glazoron crew a dumbass. He mumbled, "I'm sorry about that."

The boy giggled, looked behind them, and waved at the silent mob following them. They stopped and bowed before resuming their journey.

"In here." The captain stepped aside.

"After you," Tyler said. "I insist."

"As you wish." The captain walked through. The bridge was located forward against the inner bulkhead of the double-hulled vessel. It was big enough for a dozen crew to comfortably manage the workstations. Screens covered two-hundred and seventy degrees of the bulkhead space. They showed a live feed of the Gate, a glimpse of *Wyatt Earp*, and a whole lot of empty space.

Clodagh moved to the front, where the captain stood. "Show me how you defeated the Gate lockout," she said without any threat or emotion.

"Of course," the now-compliant captain replied. He tapped the screen and brought up a program that accessed a back door into the Gate. It shouldn't have been there, but since Glazoron and Hergin were the two planets of the Barrier Nebula that had the raw materials and technological capability to build a Gate, they'd had a hand in their Gate's construction. They had installed a back door when they built it for the Federation, but only certain officials knew of its existence—like the three high ministers.

Clodagh accessed the system, coordinated with Clevarious, and transferred the program to *Wyatt Earp*. From there, Clevarious and his freeloading band of SIs dissected the program to locate the back door and build a firewall around it, preventing further access. They then looked for similar back doors. Finding no more, they declared victory.

Tyler and Clodagh received the message at the same time.

Clodagh turned to the captain. "Looks like we're done here. I recommend you return to the planet's surface. Your mission can go forward after the Magistrate has secured her suspect."

"What about the archangel? Can he grace us with a few

moments of his time and the wisdom of his calling?" the captain requested.

Tyler hugged Dery to him and the boy flapped his wings, beating Tyler around the head until he let go. Dery fluttered away and made a loop around the bridge. He stopped in front of the captain and shared a short exchange that no one heard except the captain. The Glazoron then fell to the deck, planting his forehead on the cold steel.

Floyd nuzzled the captain's head while he was down there.

Dery returned to Tyler's arm and folded his wings behind him. *Home, please.*

"The ship *is* our home, isn't it, little man? It's probably better than we all deserve, too. Rivka makes sure of it."

Clodagh picked up Floyd, who whined because she was tired and wanted to sleep.

Rivka, Dery said. *Angry.*

"Rivka is angry?" Tyler asked while they walked. The Glazoron crew bowed while pressing themselves against the bulkheads, making way for the small group.

Angry, the boy reiterated.

"I guess we'll find out when we return, which we'll do with the utmost haste." Tyler hurried to the airlock and through.

Clodagh was breathing hard when she came through a few seconds after them. "Floyd! You're too heavy." She put the wombat down. "Clevarious, are we secure? No one came through?"

"No one. Once Dery boarded the Glazoron ship, you had a captive audience," Clevarious replied using the speakers. "What happened over there?"

Dery flew off Tyler's arm and headed toward his quarters.

"They called him 'the archangel.' They bowed to him, and when he 'talked' with the captain, the man was completely overcome. Thanks to him, we accomplished what we needed. Time to head back to the planet. Dery and I both need to see Rivka."

"Dery needs to see Rivka?" Clevarious asked. "That is an odd thing, but when he speaks, it always carries an insight that helps us."

"Exactly. Detach the airlock extension, secure the ship, and return to the spaceport if you would be so kind."

"I live to take us to spaceports. We can all get out and walk around. Well, most of us can do that."

"Snark much, Clevarious? Us poor humans have to walk around on our own two legs while you long for such a thing. Pull some strings. Move up in the queue and get yourself a hot body."

"It would be sufficiently cooled before I could occupy a SCAMP," Clevarious replied.

"No, I meant…never mind, C. Good luck working the system. Would you still fly the ship, or would one of your freeloader buddies take over?"

"You keep calling them freeloaders. They are simply here in between assignments. I think the term is 'unemployed and holding out for those who are willing to recognize their value.'"

"So, *freeloaders*," Tyler emphasized. "I can't believe there aren't jobs out there. I know there are. You need only negotiate with the employers to get what you deserve. These people flying their ships are accepting substandard performance. There's no way they're getting the most from their travels. They need an SI to do that."

"I very much agree with you, as do we all, me and the freeloaders," Clevarious said with his best colloquialized accent and phraseology.

"Are we at the spaceport yet?" Tyler asked.

"We haven't left. Clodagh is on the bridge. You should probably join her," Clevarious advised.

Tyler hurried to the bridge in time to see the Gate form. The ship headed through and reappeared just above Landing Pad Sixty-nine. The ship touched down in exactly the same spot it had been before, and the cargo ramp descended for ease of movement for the detainees. Tyler ran off the bridge.

He hoped to see Frenzik as one of those secured, but it wasn't to be. The Albions were from the ships. Spacefaring individuals, not corporate types.

Rivka strolled up behind the Albions that Red, Lewis, and Furny took to the brig. Cole was nowhere to be seen. Sahved, either.

Tyler held his hands out in the universal gesture that signified a question.

"Bagged a few criminals. Pirate captains. Clevarious tells me you have the high ministers. I'm quite pleased."

"Dery said he needs to see you." Tyler nodded at the airlock in the cargo bay.

"That sounds interesting. What happened?"

"First, if you give them the finger, it breaks the ice and is a sign of respect. The other part was Archangel Der'ayd'nil. It was the damnedest thing. You'll have to ask him about it."

"I'm sure I'll get a straight answer, too."

Tyler snorted. "There is that."

Rivka stopped in the corridor. "C, where can I find Dery?"

"In his family's quarters."

"What do you want to see him for?" Red demanded from down by the brig.

Tyler faced him, smiled, and froze.

"Dery went aboard the Glazoron ship to talk with the crew," Clevarious explained helpfully.

"He did what? Who let him board an enemy vessel?" Red glared at Tyler.

"I'll be in our quarters." Tyler took one step before Red blocked the way.

"Come on, all of you. Only Dery can make this right and put everyone's heart and mind at ease."

Red followed Tyler too closely, looming over him as they went. Rivka glanced over her shoulder and winked at Tyler.

He shook his head. "I told him no, but he was having none of it."

"You're the adult!" Red snapped.

Lindy appeared by Tyler's side. "What did you do?"

"I didn't do anything. Your son is the archangel. You should be proud and honored." Tyler clenched his jaw and raised his chin in defiance.

"Probably," Lindy conceded. She nodded at Red and gestured for him to back up.

They reached Red's and Lindy's quarters. Rivka knocked gently and opened the door to find Dery sound asleep with Floyd on Red's and Lindy's bed.

"He looks like an angel, doesn't he?" Lindy beamed at her son.

"Let me know when he's awake." Rivka clapped Red on the back. "Don't beat anyone up until after we hear what Dery has to say."

"But afterward is okay?" Red cracked his knuckles and stared at Tyler.

"Afterward won't be warranted, I suspect, so cool your jets, Milk Toast." Rivka headed toward the bridge.

"Milk Toast? Don't you mean Bristle Hound? Oh, yeah! Prime bistok, right here." Red flexed his massive biceps and struck a pose. Lindy stabbed him in his armpit with her pointer finger. He bounced off the doorway and nearly fell over in his attempt to escape.

"You're not going to let him beat me up, are you?"

"I thought you've been working out. Can't you take him yet?"

"Maybe I'm a lover and not a fighter."

"Maybe I won't allow anyone on the crew to fight, least of all Red. He doesn't need to risk getting hurt."

"You think I could hurt him? That's a lot of confidence." Tyler grinned.

"I think he might trip over your unconscious body and hit his head on the doorframe."

"That hurts me. Cuts me deep." He waited in the corridor while Rivka took the captain's seat on the bridge.

"Clevarious, did you find anything in the ship's computers that would give us insight into where Frenzik might be?"

"Nothing. We continue to parse the data, but Frenzik has gone out of his way to leave no trail."

"Access the spaceport systems and see about the shuttle he rode in. I'm going to talk with the high ministers."

Rivka popped out of her seat and strode briskly down the corridor to the conference room. She squeezed in around the high ministers.

She motioned for them to sit. "High ministers." She gave them the finger a bit awkwardly, but they brightened and returned the gesture. She had to fight not to laugh.

Red appeared in the doorway and watched closely. He still wore his body armor and carried his railgun. Rivka didn't expect anything untoward from this group, but Red was correct to join her and keep watch. He would be inconsolable if anything happened to her.

She continued, "What happened to you that your people reported you missing?"

They looked at each other but didn't answer.

"What the hell happened?" Rivka slapped her hand on the arm closest to her.

Hiding from an assassination. An order to go underground from an alien voice.

"You thought you were going to be killed? Was the alien voice that of an Albion?" Rivka pressed. Two questions got confused thoughts in response. Rivka knew better than to ask two questions so close together, but one reply came through loud and clear.

The voice was that of an Albion.

Which one? Frenzik maintained a barrier between himself and the people he coerced.

"It's good that you hid yourselves. I wouldn't put it past the individuals to harm those who defy them. That's why we're here to bring the worlds of the Barrier Nebula back to a level of good order and discipline." Rivka spoke privately with Clevarious. *I could use my team back, but the SCAMPs are on board* Destiny's Vengeance. *Do they all need to be up there?*

"We apologize for causing you and the Preeminent Supremeness any grief. We were afraid for our lives."

"Did they try to blackmail you with allegations of transgressions from your past?"

The three looked at each other again, but they didn't answer. Rivka stood so she could rest her hand on the shoulder of the one who looked the most guilty.

"What are they blackmailing you for?" she asked.

Corruption. Self-dealing. Enrichment at the people's expense.

Rivka didn't bother articulating the crimes. They were commonplace on too many worlds. She leaned against the bulkhead of the conference room and took in the three.

"Listen, you're scumbags. You've filled your personal coffers because you could when you knew you shouldn't, but you did it anyway. You deserve to be punished, but by Glazoron authorities, not me.

"Do you know why the Albions had leverage over each of you? Because all communication goes through Rising Sun Industries. Frenzik and his people have heard every private word you've spoken. We'll install a direct line to Yoll to satisfy the Federation charter, but that doesn't mean you can get away with what you've done. However, it will go much easier on you if you tell me everything you know about Rising Sun Industries. Why are they knee-deep in your business?"

Rivka knew the answer was related to Gate drives. She'd seen two Rising Sun ships sporting them, and it would be naïve to think they were the only ones. That terrified Rivka. She couldn't allow that kind of power in the hands of an individual like Malpace Frenzik, even if he had come by the technology legally.

That grated on her soul. She'd have to illegally prevent him from keeping the Gate drives. Taking them to study was one thing. Blocking him from getting them back was completely different. It crossed from the law to politics.

She'd seen his Gate's shimmer, and it was nothing like a Federation Gate's. She suspected the truth was new technology. That haunted her.

Have you found out anything about the Gate drive? Please find me something that shows stolen Federation technology in there, she privately pleaded with Clodagh.

Working on it, Magistrate. I could use some help.

Clevarious, recall Destiny's Vengeance. *Beg them to return and help us dissect this Gate drive we pulled from* Rising Sun.

I shall pass on your request, Clevarious replied.

"Where is Frenzik?" Rivka asked. "I don't want any of your bullshit. I know everything you've done and that you were running to save your own miserable hides. Real leaders stand up to bullies like Malpace Frenzik. They don't run with their ill-gotten gains and turn over their people to someone like him. You should be fucking ashamed of yourselves."

"We don't know where he is. We've been in hiding. No contact with anyone until we were able to book passage on the executive cruiser."

Lindy arrived and tapped Red on the shoulder. She whispered into his ear, and he nodded in reply.

"Let me reframe my question. Where did you last see

Frenzik, and where might he be? You know who he's trying to manipulate. You know what contracts he's trying to get signed. Tell me before I throw you three in the brig with the three Albions already stuffed in there."

"You have Albions on this ship?" one of the high ministers cried in alarm.

"They're in the brig. They will know nothing about your presence unless you want them to. As in, don't answer my questions, and you'll be getting up close and personal with your soon-to-be bestest buddies."

The first Glazoron high minister waved his middle digit at Rivka. She nearly came out of her seat to rip his finger from his hand before she remembered. That was his way of conceding.

"Where?"

"We met Frenzik and his team at the ministry's center in the Glazira Cyber Trunk, the area bordering our tech industry's manufacturing center. There is a meeting facility that is large enough to accommodate the grossly oversized Albions. He wanted a fifty-one percent stake in the facilities, all of them. We couldn't oblige him even if we had wanted to because they are privately owned, although most of the work is for the government."

A second minister continued because the first looked spent. "He told us to cancel the government contracts and pressure them into signing new agreements that would give the result he had asked for: Rising Sun Industries control over Glazoron high-tech manufacturing.

"His Supreme Preeminence rejected the proposals outright, even going so far as to call the negotiations a complete waste of time. It was a bold move. Mister Frenzik did not appear pleased by the revelation. He said that he would return in a week to present a new offer. It was that night that our lives were threatened. The week is up today."

"Today? You mean Frenzik has a scheduled meeting that he is supposed to attend?"

"Yes. What time is it?" the minister asked.

"It's one in the afternoon, local time," Clevarious stated.

The ministers looked for the source of the voice, and Rivka explained, "The sentient intelligence running the ship. He knows what there is to know."

"Ah, yes. We have an AI that handles that, but he's old and could use an infusion of energy."

CHAPTER SIXTEEN

***Wyatt Earp*, Landing Pad Sixty-nine, Glazoron Spaceport**
"We have a small group of currently unemployed sentient intelligences. That's a different name for AI, but these individuals are different. They have full individual rights. What about your AI? Does he have rights and an employment contract?"

"A what? No. It's a program, nothing more."

"We'll talk with your AI and determine his or her status. Clevarious?"

"Already passed to the embassy of the Singularity for action. They will be here momentarily."

"There we go. They have their own embassy. Did you know that?"

"Computer programs have an embassy?"

"They are sentient. We don't keep sentient creatures as pets or slaves. I'd say you didn't know and let it go, but we'll see if Frenzik shows up to his meeting. I'll need you to stay here while we take care of business."

"We could go. We'll arrange our own transportation."

"If you aren't willing to stay in this room, we could throw you in the brig with the Albions. Those are your only two choices. Here or brig. Never mind. I'll decide for you. Stay here."

Rivka slapped the table before showing herself out and closing the door behind her. She found Red, Lindy, and Dery waiting. The boy pointed at the conference room.

"I'm not sure you want to go in there, little man. Then again, you already know who's in there and what you need to do."

The boy smiled.

"What happened on board the Glazoron ship?" Rivka asked.

They know the legends of my people. They know, Dery replied.

"Your other people are a bunch of confused do-gooders on board *Wyatt Earp*. I know you understand that you are loved, and we would do anything for you. Just tell us what," Rivka said while resting her hand on his shoulder. She enjoyed the feeling of calm he radiated through her. His was the only soul she'd ever touched that was completely pure. From before he was born, he had been a positive influence on everyone he met.

He cupped Rivka's cheek in his small hand. *I know.*

She had no idea what that was in relation to, and she didn't try to decipher it. "I love you, little man."

Lindy and Red stared. "Did he tell you what happened?"

"In his own way, yes. I'm sorry. I thought you heard."

"He doesn't always share with everyone," Lindy said. "He says what he needs to say only to those who need to hear."

Rivka nodded. She pointed at Red's face. "You're not going to beat Tyler up. You're going to apologize and stop being a wiener to him. Do you understand me?"

"Did Dery tell you that?"

"I told me that. I need to keep the peace on this ship, and you're damaging my calm."

"I don't want to damage your calm," Red mumbled. Dery giggled and poked his father's nose.

"Make sure they stay in there," Rivka told Lindy. "Red, you're with me. We're going to catch Frenzik if he finds it in his heart to come to the meeting he committed to. Two hours to show time, which means we need to go now." Rivka yelled toward the bridge, "Cloak the ship and take us to the Glazira Cyber Trunk!"

Rivka shot to her quarters to get her Magistrate's jacket. Red waited for her in the corridor. The Albions in the brig were making noise.

"Clevarious, can you deliver sleeping gas to those idiots?" Red asked.

"I'll put them out of your misery, Vered. For a brief time, that is," Clevarious replied.

Rivka elbowed Red in the midsection, but it was a wasted effort since he still wore ballistic protection.

Tyler lifted his chin by way of greeting. Red responded in kind.

Rivka hurried toward the bridge. She walked as if she had all the time in the world. She kept glancing at Red, who kept his distance.

"What?" he asked.

"Are you appropriately chastised?"

"I guess, whatever that means. I'm jiggy."

"You're who?" Rivka stopped to look at him. He threw up his hands in surrender. She turned back to the bridge. "Never mind. We've got a Frenzik to catch!"

"First arrest. I forgot to report that one," Red said.

"I documented it," Clevarious offered with panache. "We are up on the betting lines. All we need is the main suspect in cuffs, begging for mercy!"

"Too true, C. Bring me the head of Alfredo Garcia."

"I cannot until I get my SCAMP. Then I shall hunt down the Alfredos of the Garcia to satisfy your challenge."

"I lost you, Magistrate," Red said. "Do you have a new suspect?"

"No. It was me humoring myself. The head I want to see on a platter is that of Malpace Frenzik. I bet this time he'll call me honey or his little love pumpkin or something equally demeaning."

"Do you want me to add it as a betting line?" Red looked hopeful.

"No!" Rivka waved him away and leaned on the back of the captain's chair.

Clodagh was in the seat with an uncharacteristically docile Tiny Man Titan on her lap. The ship angled skyward and raced above the buildings on its way to the Cyber Trunk. "How we playing this, Magistrate?"

Rivka blew out her breath through pursed lips and stared at the screen. "Clevarious, bring up a map of the area."

The requested overview appeared on the main screen. The Cyber Trunk was big, dominating the lesser buildings on the campus.

It towered over the others, but it was separate. "When

we get there, scan the ground looking for tunnels or underground exits of any sort. We need to isolate him and cut him off from escape."

"We'll work up an egress map by the time we get there," Clevarious promised.

"Is *Destiny's Vengeance* tethered?" Rivka wondered.

"They're flying above us and will join us when we reach the Trunk."

"Good. I need my whole team together, and we need the embassy to get on the issue of a supposed *AI* running things. He needs to be granted his citizenship and freedom if he is indeed sentient and elevated to the lofty status of SI and citizen of the Singularity."

"For which we thank you, Magistrate, for securing our rights before all of the Federation."

"Toot sweet," Rivka replied.

Red screwed his face up in confusion. Rivka laughed.

"You say the damnedest things." He shook his head.

Wyatt Earp looped around the Trunk, scanning and ingesting every bit of geospatial information it could collect to build a three-dimensional diagram of the facility.

"One tunnel which connects to the next building. We can secure that from the termination side in the smaller building. Otherwise, above-ground routes from each of the four sides. Multiple doors throughout. A landing pad on the roof. And that's it."

"There are more exits than we can cover. Have Cole report to the bridge."

"He's still in his armored suit but is on his way," Clevarious confirmed.

He shuffled down the corridor, blocking it for anyone else.

"Don't we have a cat?" Rivka asked out of the blue.

Clodagh pointed at the pilot's station. Underneath was a bed with extra fur and a cushion. Wenceslaus was his typical orange self, resting sphinxlike and staring at Tiny Man Titan.

Cole announced his arrival. "You rang?"

"Take a look at the map. We think Frenzik is either in there or coming. I, of course, want him boxed in so we can take him into custody. What do you recommend for a tactical plan?"

"It would depend on if he's there already or not. If not, then we'd have to hide until after he arrived." Cole remained in the corridor but used his suit's enhanced optics and interface to move the three-dimensional map so he could better study it on his heads-up display.

"That's my concern. He's not there. *Wyatt Earp* is cloaked. If we land on the roof and he flies in, he'll get a surprise when he bumps against our hull. If we drop off your warriors, then you'll have to find a place to hide while wearing your combat armor."

"We could go without the armor," Cole suggested. "We'd be stressed with the oversized railguns, but if we aren't carrying packs or other encumbrances, we'll be fine. Our whole role is to bag this one Albion? We can do that because he's an asshole."

"What's his being an asshole have to do with it?" Red asked. "Not that I disagree."

"Extra effort for those who deserve it. We'll go stripped down if need be," Cole explained.

"If he has henchmen, as evil supervillains are wont to have, then your combat armor will come in handy to eliminate the ancillary threat. Go in with full gear. Stay out of sight around the buildings here, here, and here." Rivka pointed at three spots on the map. "And put one warrior at the exit to the tunnel leading into the Trunk."

"One there, and we can watch three sides. We can get anywhere we need to pretty quickly. That leaves one side uncovered. I'd pick this one. Sahved and Tyler can watch it. You, Red, and Lindy go inside and make the collar."

Rivka spoke slowly. "The collar. We don't have much on him. I don't have enough to send him to Jhiordaan, but I can hit his company with the highest fines possible for perverting the required comm channels. It's weak, I know. He's thrown so many credits at taking over these planets that he probably is operating Rising Sun at a loss, so I can't get him for tax evasion, but that wouldn't be a Federation problem. Do we have anything on that Gate drive yet?"

Clodagh laughed. "I haven't been back there, and we don't have our technical experts Ankh and Erasmus. They'll reboard shortly. It's only been five minutes since you last wondered about it."

Rivka sulked briefly. "We better not land. Hover where Cole indicated and prep Sahved and Tyler to be eyeballs-only watch. They go unarmed. I'm not going to commit them to a firefight. All they have to do is call Cole or his people, who can be there in seconds." She pointed down. "Deploy the troops."

"What the hell?" Tyler bellowed from down the corridor. "Sahved!"

"I'm guessing you let him know." Rivka glanced over her shoulder and yelled at the corridor, "Take extra water."

"We're going to talk about this when I get back," Tyler replied.

"No sex if we do," Rivka shouted back.

Tyler didn't continue his contention.

Red bit his lip and waited. "Man Candy is smarter than he looks."

"He looks plenty smart," Rivka said as she continued to study the screen. "We might as well go, too. We'll walk in through the front door like we own the place."

"I like that plan," Red replied. He slapped Blazer's hand guard and turned to Lindy. "Let's rock and roll. I can't wait to get my hands on Frenzik. I hate that guy."

"As much as I want to remain neutral, I'm having a hard time." Rivka stepped away from the captain's chair. "Let's see if he shows up. Hold down the fort, Clodagh. We'll be back."

Rivka strolled down the corridor, giving the others time to climb out and deploy. They were a little under two hours early.

"I hope we beat him here," Rivka mumbled.

Red ran down the ramp. Sahved and Tyler scampered away. The warriors used their pneumatic jets to fly to their observation points to avoid pounding the ground with their heavy tread.

Rivka continued walking casually. It helped her feel like she was in charge. In every engagement with Frenzik, he did his best to belittle the Magistrate and establish dominance. This time, there was nothing to discuss. They'd arrest him for his minor crimes and expand, depending on what Rivka learned during the "interrogation."

She wanted to know his strategic goals. Why did he want control over the Barrier Nebula? The answer to that question would illuminate the path to stop him and Rising Sun Industries.

It begged the question of whether they needed to be stopped. They were doing great things for each planet.

The immensity of the goodwill versus the loss of freedoms pulled her in opposite directions. She wanted to hammer him while also wanting to keep his philanthropic efforts intact. She'd been thinking about it but hadn't come to any resolution. She'd take care of the first part before worrying about the second part.

That gave her a level of internal satisfaction and calm that resulted in pangs of guilt. She didn't like the feeling.

She wanted to gloat, but it wasn't time for that.

They walked in the front door exactly as Rivka wanted —like they owned the place. *Where are we going, C?*

Chaz and Dennicron are on their way to you. They have the building's layout, Clevarious replied.

"We'll wait for the rest of the team," Rivka stated. She twiddled her thumbs for a few seconds before Chaz and Dennicron showed up.

They waved as they walked by. They headed upstairs and continued to the top floor. They found the meeting room empty.

Rivka wanted something in this case to go easily. She had gotten her hopes up, and now she was disappointed.

Red saw the look on her face. "No joy, Magistrate. We're going to have to do this the hard way. And what kind of freak shows up two hours early for a *meeting?*" The word rolled distastefully off his tongue, and he worked his jaw like he wanted to spit.

"Looks like we're going to have to wait," Rivka conceded. *All hands, keep me informed.*

She took a seat at the big table that filled the room. She faced the doorway. She slapped her datapad down in front of her. Red and Lindy assumed positions on either side of the door. They leaned against the wall and relaxed with their hands on their railguns, ready for immediate action.

After ten minutes, Lindy dragged a chair to the wall and sat down. Red continued to stand but tapped his foot. Thirty minutes, then an hour. Red peeked out the door.

Any movement? Rivka asked, knowing there had been none. Her team would have reported anything.

We have Frenzik in custody and are sipping beers on board Wyatt Earp, Cole replied.

Rivka almost rose to the bait, but she caught herself halfway out of her seat. *What I hear you saying is that you haven't seen anything.*

Nothing at all. This place is a ghost town, Cole reported.

You're going to get your ass kicked, Cole, Red interjected.

Clevarious, scan the media and comm channels, looking for any surge of security or meetings that have been moved from the Trunk," Rivka requested.

We've been doing that. We have no joy. The good news is that we are having a robust and enlightening conversation with Killmouskie, the SI who runs this place. They have him shackled. He didn't know anything about the Singularity or the existence of others like him. We'll liberate him from the chains of his slavery the second you have Frenzik in custody. And no, he doesn't know where Frenzik is. He has limited access to strategic issues.

What a waste, Rivka replied. *Educate him on what signs of Frenzik look like. I'm sure he's seen something. Redirections. Securing facilities. Things that would make no sense without the privacy component. Cockroaches hiding from the light.*

Good point, Magistrate. We'll take care of that, Clevarious promised.

Rivka spoke aloud. "Cole needs to have his ass kicked, but then again, it's something I would do when the answer was obvious to a question that didn't need to be asked. He's off the hook because we taught him his sense of humor. Touché!"

Red just nodded. He was tense. With each passing second, his anticipation of a confrontation with the Albion grew.

CHAPTER SEVENTEEN

Glazira Cyber Trunk, Glazoron

Fifteen minutes before the set time for the meeting, three Glazorons walked into the room. They slowed when they saw Rivka and stopped cold when their eyes fell on Red and Lindy.

"What is this?" one asked.

Rivka stood. "I'm Magistrate Rivka Anoa, and I've invited myself to your meeting because I'm interested in one of the others who is supposed to attend."

"This is a private meeting," the individual pressed.

"If that were the case, then I wouldn't be here. Who are you expecting?"

The speaker went silent, no longer willing to ask or answer questions. He turned to leave, but Lindy blocked the door. She motioned at the table with the barrel of her railgun. Rivka strolled around the table and rested her hand on the round and soft arm of the Glazoron who had done all the talking.

"I asked you who's coming. Frenzik?"

An image of the CEO of Rising Sun Industries appeared in the industry professional's mind. High-tech manufacture. The mass production of Gate drives.

"This is going to be a problem. The Federation can't allow civilian production of Gate drives. Not yet. They're discussing it at the Federation level among the ambassadors."

"Doesn't affect me. How did you know?"

"We know everything. What other crimes have you committed?" Rivka asked.

The individual's mind was clear. He hadn't committed any crimes as far as he knew. He was an upstanding citizen. A family man but shrewd in the ways of business.

"I haven't committed any crimes. I follow the law! There is no law restricting Gate technology. Making a deal with an intergalactic corporation is good business."

"You mean Rising Sun Industries?" Rivka wanted him to give her something.

"Of course I mean Rising Sun Industries. They have the clout to guarantee a consistent supply chain. Hergin raw materials are always a testy proposition, but according to Rising Sun, the deal for what we need has been struck. The only remaining factor is to sign the contract."

"What does Rising Sun get beside Gate drives? Do they get ownership of your companies or a leadership role in planetary government? There has to be more."

"Guaranteed payment for each Gate drive produced that is quite substantial, even though Rising Sun provided the complete design and manufacturing process. Our contract is exclusive, but the initial order for one hundred drives will take years to complete. We will continue ratcheting up production until we grow short of raw materials."

"A hundred!" Rivka's eyes darted around the room as she tried to wrap her head around the implications. "How many have you already delivered?"

"Three," the man answered proudly.

Rivka's lip twitched. *Clevarious, there are three total Gate drives out there. Let everyone know that we can account for two.*

We'll spread the word.

Rivka needed to talk it through. *If he gave the first one to himself and the second one to his pirate cruiser, who got the third one, since he didn't put one on the drone carrier? Or did he, and it's not operational? If he didn't, what would be the next most important ship that needed to move quickly anywhere in the galaxy?*

No one had an answer.

Cole interrupted her thoughts. *An Albion delegation has just arrived. I can't tell if Frenzik is with them.*

"Now we're getting somewhere." Rivka nodded at Red and Lindy.

They nodded back. Lindy pushed the chair out of the way to clear the space around her. Red flexed and stretched. "What's the plan?"

"Get them into the room and secure them until we can figure out who's who and what they're here for. If Frenzik is with them, take him into custody first. I'll get my interrogation my way."

Wyatt Earp tracked the Albion delegation's travel up the stairs to the top floor. When the door opened, there were no surprises. The first Albion ducked to enter the room.

He stopped once inside, blocking the other two in his party.

"Please come in, all of you," Rivka said.

Red grabbed the first one's arm and yanked him toward the table. He wanted to see if Frenzik was behind him. After he took a good look at the other two, he snarled, "Not Frenzik. Assholeman."

"I thought he was on his way to Finx?" Rivka raised her voice. "Get in here, Ahsooleyman. I expect you have Belloward with you, don't you?"

The Albion she'd sent to Jhiordaan stepped through the doorway and cleared the space so Belloward could join them. Lindy closed the door after them.

"Where's Frenzik?" Rivka asked.

"Wouldn't you like to know?" Ahsooleyman replied.

Rivka nodded tightly. "I would." She walked around the table to face the Albion. His head nearly touched the ceiling while standing upright, forcing her to look up to see his face. Her hand shot out to grip his wrist. *"Where's Frenzik?"* she shouted.

The embassy. That was the one place he could stay and be safe. Rivka had crossed enough ambassadors to know that she couldn't remove him with impunity, no matter what the Federation charter said about the authority of the High Chancellor and his Magistrates.

"Well, now. How was your stay in Jhiordaan?" She continued to hold his wrist.

She recoiled at the nightmares that coursed through his mind. Despite his size, he wasn't violent enough to weather the attacks upon his person. He and Belloward had suffered greatly. Rivka stepped back. "No threats. I want

Frenzik. Are you willing to go back to Jhiordaan to protect him? You know he's the one who should have been incarcerated. It was all Frenzik."

The lights shone in his eyes as he considered it. Rivka had sent him to prison once. She could do it again.

Belloward looked frantically for an escape route. Jhiordaan was the last thing he wanted to discuss.

"Immunity," Rivka offered. "You don't want to go back there, and I don't want to send you. There's a way you can make sure that doesn't happen."

Ahsooleyman's emotions crisscrossed his face as he contemplated the offer. Frenzik's power was significant, and his hold on his people was nearly absolute.

The battle raging within the Albion suggested there were cracks in Frenzik's hold. Loyalty was his trademark currency.

Rivka continued. "We know he's at the Albion Embassy. Encourage him to come out. That's all I want, and we'll let the legal process work after that. Right now, I don't have a lot except the intimidation of planetary governments, maintaining a private pirate fleet, running a protection racket, and interfering with the Federation charter. Stuff like that. It's not enough to be considered a capital crime. He'll earn his stripes in Jhiordaan, but not for too long. Just long enough for us to dismantle Rising Sun Industries to eliminate the monopoly they've established."

"Mister Frenzik didn't do any of that stuff," Ahsooleyman said after taking a big breath. He smiled weakly as he started to find his spine. As much as he didn't want to return to Jhiordaan, he didn't want to cross Frenzik. His fear of one did not outweigh his fear of the other.

Just like that, her advantage was gone.

"You," she said to the first Albion, poking him with her index finger. "What's *your* claim to fame?"

"I find your tone offensive," he replied.

Ahsooleyman nudged him and shook his head almost imperceptibly.

Maybe she hadn't lost *all* her leverage. Ahsooleyman had been a raging asshole during Rising Sun's attempt to take Lewbamar over by inciting an insurrection. How he had been released was beyond Rivka. The fire behind his eyes wasn't so confrontational.

"My name is Grossmon. I am in charge of technological operations for Rising Sun Industries. Our collaboration with Hergin and Glazoron is beneficial from both business and governmental perspectives. We all win with technology that frees us from the constraints of the Federation Gate system."

"There was a time when the Gates were considered an engineering marvel. They gave freedom, not took it away," Rivka replied.

The Albions made no move to sit. They continued to stand by the door, ready for a rapid exit should the opportunity present itself.

"You're a little young to have first-hand memories, but your understanding of history is acceptable."

Rivka didn't care if he accepted her understanding of history. "Where are the three Gate drives you've already received?"

"On ships," Grossmon replied.

"How serendipitous!" Rivka blurted. "That's where we put ours, too. Wow. What a small universe."

Grossmon stared at her.

Rivka showed her cards. "*Rising Sun*. The pirate cruiser. Where's the third one?" The cruiser's drive had been dismantled. The key parts were on *Wyatt Earp*, along with the entire drive from *Rising Sun*. She didn't feel bad about that. She didn't care how much Frenzik had spent to get them, although the credits had to have come from the planets Frenzik had been exploiting to build his empire.

There was a method to his machinations.

A supply chain to deliver food, raw materials, technology, and labor—everything he needed to establish dominance. But he already had that with Rising Sun. He seemed to have an endless appetite for more. For business conquest on a galactic scale.

It wasn't just business.

"Where is Frenzik building his army?" Rivka asked.

The Albions looked at each other. "Army?" Grossmon asked.

Rivka took him by the forearm. "Yes. Army. A military for the conquest of this sector, then the entire Federation. Albions. A race of giants that will crush us underfoot."

Ahsooleyman half-smiled. "I fear you've gone off the deep end, Magistrate. Mister Frenzik and Rising Sun Industries are only interested in free trade between the planets of the Barrier Nebula, with a modest expansion when market conditions are amenable."

"Listen to you, spouting the corporate business line. If it was all about free trade, the second Gate drive wouldn't have gone to a pirate cruiser. It would have gone to a freighter."

"Alas, during the trial phase, I expect we didn't wish to

lose any freight." He turned to the door. "If that's all, we'll be on our way."

"You don't care to sign the contract with these good people?" Rivka asked. "How about you take your seats? We're a long way from being finished."

"We *are* finished, Magistrate." Grossmon glared at Lindy. "Please, move."

"Would you like a ride to your embassy?" Rivka asked.

"We'll manage." He leaned back to tap the nearest Glazoron on the shoulder. "Join us at our embassy, where we'll sign the contracts. This area has become too unsavory for such a joyous occasion. We will celebrate with Benjo Beer and diatribes." The Albion thought for a moment. He raised his hand and gave them the finger, making sure not to wave it in Rivka's direction.

The Glazoron executives responded in kind. Rivka did too, holding her middle digit high and steady.

"See? There is no room for animosity. Let us sign the contracts now," the Glazoron said. He was in a nearly euphoric state.

"Albion Embassy in two hours. We will see you there."

At Rivka's nod, Lindy stepped aside.

Red snarled like a wild animal denied its prey.

The Albions departed, and the Glazoron followed them out.

Rivka was both relieved and insulted that they didn't give her the finger.

"You're going to just let them go?" Red asked.

Rivka silenced him with a cold look. "Focus. We want Frenzik. I don't have anything on those three. I'd love to throw them back in the gray bar motel, but vengeance doesn't justify it. We have to be above reproach."

"I know," Red apologized. "It's just frustrating."

"You're not telling me anything I don't know. Let's get back to the ship. I want good news on that Gate drive. I want to hear that it contains stolen technology so we can slam the door shut on this whole Hergin-Glazoron-Rising Sun unholy alliance."

CHAPTER EIGHTEEN

<u>Wyatt Earp, Hovering above the Albion Embassy, Glazoron</u>

Ankh maintained his emotionless expression. "It's all original technology, but it's a good fifteen years behind Federation Gates. It needs more energy than the power source can supply, so it has to be tied into a ship's engine, where it will draw power from other systems, like the sublight drives. *Rising Sun* had an additional reactor beyond the one dedicated to the Gate drive. Otherwise, they would have only managed one jump before we caught them dead in space. As it was, it only took four before they could no longer Gate."

"I need to report this to the High Chancellor. Thanks, Ankh. Can we defeat this Gate drive with a pulse or a weapon of some sort?"

"Working on it," Ankh replied. He shooed Rivka out of the engineering space.

She needed different answers than the one she'd just heard. She walked quickly to her quarters, then disappeared into the hologrid. Tyler was fresh out of the shower and naked. He started dancing, knowing she could see him through a gap in the screens.

"I'm going to turn the camera on you," Rivka promised.

"Don't put Grainger off his game," Tyler replied. He turned on some music.

"This is serious!"

"It always is. You'll handle it. You've already planted the seed. That was last week. Now you have confirmation. The cat is out of the bag."

"A hundred cats," Rivka replied. She dropped the hologrid without making the call. "This is a complete shit sandwich. A creature like Frenzik with Gate drive technology. He's building an army; I can feel it in my bones. He's using the twelve planets as his army supply store. Just look at what he's compiled."

"If that's the case, then he has surely broken the law. Insurrection against the Federation will not be tolerated. He'll bring the entire might of the Federation down around Rising Sun's ears. What if it's colonialism, as in, they're looking to expand beyond the Barrier Nebula into uncharted space?"

"I fear Frenzik has that justification dialed up, but I don't see him coveting places that can't bow to his greatness."

"Narcissism. Is that his sole driving force?" Tyler wondered.

"It's driven greater men than him. I need to get my hands on him so I can learn the truth." She brought the hologrid back up. Tyler moved off to get dressed. Rivka made the call.

"Look at you, calling me in the middle of the day. What did you find out?" Grainger asked in greeting.

"The Gate drive is original technology. The Glazoron have delivered three of them, but we can only account for two, and it's worse. Frenzik has an order in for a hundred of them."

"Not sure it can get much worse than that. The Federation Council is deliberating a proposed law regarding Gate drives on ships, but there's a lot of resistance to an outright ban. I don't think we're going to be able to put this djinni back in the bottle." Grainger rubbed his chin while frowning. "It's not a crime to develop groundbreaking technology."

"Frightfully so," Rivka replied. "I have a gut feeling that he's building an army to attack Federation assets."

"That's a whole different issue. What evidence do you have to support this claim?"

Rivka's dour expression was the answer Grainger had expected.

"Nothing, then. We'll keep this line of inquiry to ourselves. Uncover some hard evidence to support your conclusion. We can bring a small army of accountants and overseers to put a crimp in his plans and maybe even stop them cold. We can deploy the Federation's own army. We'll see how the Albions fare against our hermaphrodites. I'm assuming the soldiers are Albion. It wouldn't be very intimidating if they were the tiny bear people of Lewbamar."

"They have a name, Grainger."

"I know."

"Tiny bear people. They weren't very frightening until

they stampeded into the exercise yard. Then they were nothing but claws and teeth."

"They're not fighters. At three meters tall, the Albions would cut a striking pose on the battlefield."

"They'll also be really big targets, but we're digressing. Legally, we're stymied until they show their hand. I have some minor stuff on Frenzik, but it's little more than a pile of misdemeanors. As much as I hate the guy, I can't bend the law to send him to Jhiordaan, as much as I want to. I need to interrogate him my way."

Grainger knew what she meant. "You have hunches, but do you have enough for a search warrant that will stand up to the scrutiny of the Federation Council?"

"Probably not."

"Frenzik has become a favorite cause for a growing number. If it's anything less than waterproof, it'll get thrown out."

"So, our decisions can be appealed if someone has enough horsepower to get it before the council. By the way, he's holed up in his embassy. I can't touch him, literally or figuratively."

"I'll pass on the information about the Gate drive. Every planet is going to want them. Have we become Frenzik's greatest sales force?"

Rivka scowled. "Why'd you have to put it that way? Once the councilors know there are Gate drives to be had, they'll open their coffers and deal. Frenzik won't need an army except to carry the treasure away from everyone else's castle. This is dire."

"You know the old saying: 'Knowledge is power.' Our

man Frenzik has it and is going to put it up for sale. He's building an army of debt collectors."

"Maybe that's what I missed. Not an army in the normal sense but a group that will take over Federation planets nevertheless. Will they even know that they've sacrificed freedoms for progress? I need to think. I'll call back if I come up with anything else."

"Thanks, Rivka. I'm with you in that I don't want this one to get away, but the case needs to be rock-solid, with real evidence."

Rivka waved. "I hear you loud and clear. Rivka out." She closed the channel and dropped the hologrid.

Tyler was waiting for her with a giant mocha.

"I think I'd prefer a beer."

"Coming right up." Tyler set the mocha in the food processor for recycling and ordered a dark beer with chocolate undertones.

She drank half of it before she looked at it. "New recipe based on a Terry Henry brew?"

Tyler shrugged. "Ankh programs it. I have no idea what the magic behind the panel is."

"Do you have any ideas on how to get Frenzik out of the embassy?"

"I'm always up for a good plague or a toxic cloud."

"Toxic cloud. Risk of hurting innocent people is too great. Dammit!"

"Are you sure you have to go straight at him?" Tyler crossed his arms and waited patiently. Rivka shook her head. "Rising Sun main corporate. If they've been funneling all Barrier Nebula planet communications through that building, you'd have probable cause to pretty much dismantle the entire facility."

"Maybe you don't have to know how to program a food processor, but look how smart you've gotten by sleeping with a barrister. He'll come out if we shut down his corporate empire. He'll have to do something. He's not one to sit by and see his world destroyed. Good plan. Our toxic cloud will be highly targeted and hit him right in the heart."

Rivka left their quarters. "Clodagh, plot a course to Albion, best possible speed. But first, let me drop a search warrant on their embassy here. Send a hearty message to our boy Frenzik."

She hurried to the bridge, and Clodagh surrendered the captain's chair. "Clevarious, a search warrant, please, based on the perversion of Barrier Nebula's planetary communications. We know they're going through Rising Sun Industries, based on the blackmail attempts on senior officials. Efrahim, Finx, and Glazoron, to start with. All the others that don't have a direct link to Yoll, too. We're going to war, lawyer-style."

The search warrant scrolled across the screen. It was a simple document but held great power. The search was for any and all communications that should have been privileged between member planets and the Federation. It was broad, allowing her to check any and all digital communications that passed through Rising Sun Industries' corporate headquarters.

"Transmit a copy to the Albion embassy here. We'll deliver the one on Albion in person. Are we ready to Gate?"

"Intra-atmospheric Gate plotted and set in."

"Would you look at that?" Rivka said. A small vessel lifted off from behind the embassy and raced skyward.

"After that ship, if you would be so kind, Clodagh."

Clodagh tapped Kennedy on the shoulder. The pilot was already hammering the keys and bending *Wyatt Earp* to her will. Clevarious could have flown the ship, but Rivka liked the personal interface. Humans' intuition was better when it came to changing plans.

"Can we overtake it?"

"We could Gate in front of it, but this one is setting a speed record. Little ship with a big engine." Clodagh looked knowingly at Rivka.

"You think we found our third Gate drive?" Rivka asked. She suspected they both knew the answer. "If we try to disable that ship, we could destroy it. That would be a career-ending move, based on Frenzik's popularity in the Council. Let's get to Albion before them. Abandon the chase. Gate us to Albion."

"New calculations are in place. Gate forming." *Wyatt Earp* slowed to establish the wormhole. The ship slipped through and appeared above the Rising Sun Industries' corporate building.

"Nicely done! Clevarious, cut all comm lines in and out of that facility."

"Magistrate! That's a tall order. We're going to need a physical intervention. Heating up the ion cannon to cut two separate fiber trunks. The rest can be shut down through active jamming, but we'll have to remain airborne."

"That's damn inconvenient! Drop us off on the ground

and get back into the air. Cloak the ship and let me know when Frenzik arrives." Rivka activated the intercom. "All hands, prepare to deploy into the Rising Sun building. If we're successful, this could be the last time the sun rises on them."

"Fire!" Clevarious shouted. The ion cannon belched two rounds that slammed through the pavement and concrete casings to destroy the wiring within. Two hardened trunk lines into and out of the building, destroyed at the speed of heat.

"Dropoff in ten," Clodagh called.

"Woohoo. We're going in," Rivka shouted.

"Dammit!" Red bellowed from the corridor in front of his quarters. "Give a guy more than ten seconds. I was taking care of business."

"Too much information, Red. We're going to bring Frenzik to us."

"Why would he come to us? We riffle his office and upset his people."

"We cut his link to his empire with no sign that we're going to turn it back on. He loses his ability to influence those other planets. He's going to come. Plus, I think he's already on his way."

Red cheered. "Eat a bucket of dicks, you fuck."

"Vered!" Lindy shouted.

"Sorry," a chastised Red replied.

The flutter of wings followed them down the corridor. "No, little sweetheart, you can't come with us."

Coming, the boy replied for all to hear.

"These aren't the Glazoron. They won't revere you like they should," Lindy replied.

Dery was oblivious to counterarguments.

"Magistrate?" Lindy summoned support.

"He knows more than we do. When he says he's coming, I'm not sure I have the authority to tell him no. I will caution you, Dery, to stay behind your mom. Can you do that for me?"

Yes.

They all breathed a sigh of relief.

"Why do you want to come with us, sweetheart?" Lindy asked. Her son just giggled in reply.

Rivka and Red locked eyes. They were caught in the tidal wave that was Der'ayd'nil, and they surrendered to the inevitability of it.

Rivka looked down as she whispered to no one in particular, "Kill anyone who threatens the boy."

"You don't have to tell me that, but it's nice to have your blessing. I will let no harm come to my son. It's not like we can tell him he can't come when that would be my first choice."

"Mine, too. Let's execute this search warrant and see what kind of havoc we can wreak." Rivka took a step but couldn't go farther. She kneeled before Dery. "Please, little man, stay on the ship with Clodagh and Alanna. We have to do things that you shouldn't see. They may not take it kindly. I can't promise you that you can go next time, either. We're possibly going to be dealing with extreme violence. It'll be safest for all of us if you're not there. I hope you're right in thinking that you have something important to do, but I'm also convinced that you can do it from here."

Dery fluttered down to hug Rivka. He said nothing, just turned and flew toward the bridge.

"New orders, Red. Don't kill anybody who doesn't try to kill you first." Rivka clenched her jaw and turned to the cargo bay. "Let's go."

CHAPTER NINETEEN

<u>Rising Sun Industries' Corporate Headquarters, Albion</u>

Rivka strode toward the front door while an invisible *Wyatt Earp* dusted off and headed skyward to assume the best position to jam communications coming from the tower. It also gave the ship a vantage point from which to watch for Frenzik's small ship.

Red moved in front of the Magistrate to slow her down. Sahved, Chaz, and Dennicron walked behind the Magistrate, and Lindy brought up the rear. Cole and his squad deployed around the building, covering the ground-level exits.

Rivka glanced at one of two smoking holes in the pavement where a fiber-optic trunk was located.

"Sucks to be them, fixing that," Rivka said under her breath. She braced herself to face the enormity of the task before them. A thousand employees, far more than her and her team, were unable to do their jobs. There was going to be anger and probably violence. Rivka and her small team could be overwhelmed at a level that would make the Lewbamar prison debacle look like a walk on the beach.

"Do we have to wait until they try to kill us first?" Red reiterated.

"We'll play it by ear. If we shoot first, I'll make the call," Rivka replied.

The Albions in the lobby looked none too pleased. An administrative assistant Rivka recognized from their previous trip into the building approached. "Is this your doing?" she demanded.

Rivka held up her datapad. "I have a warrant to search these premises for any communications from the governments of Bretastan, Colay, Delgo, Efrahim, Finx, Glazoron, Hergin, Ypswich, Jilk, Klarber, and Lewbamar that were intended for the Federation. I have substantial evidence suggesting official communications were re-routed through this building before being retransmitted."

"We didn't do any of that." She crossed her arms and planted her feet.

"Someone here did all of that. Maybe it wasn't you, specifically. Maybe it was. You know what I've learned in all my years of dealing with perps?"

"Perps?"

"Perpetrators. Criminals. They always say they didn't do it. They lie. Consequently, I have to assume that you are lying to protect yourself and the corporation. It's okay. I don't need your testimony. I will have access to all the computers in this building, starting with the servers located at the comm node."

"All the computers? There's a zillion of them."

"It could take a while. You might as well relax or go

home. I don't care which, but you can't be on your computer during this search. Actually, no one can be on their computer. If you can let them know, I'd appreciate it."

Rivka expected her to avoid making the notification, but she didn't ignore Rivka. She returned to her desk, accessed the intrabuilding communication system, and then made the announcement. "To my delightfully successful co-workers of Rising Sun Industries. A Federation Magistrate is currently executing a search warrant to dig through our digital files. This harpy said we're not supposed to be on our computers. Stay or go home; the choice is up to individual supervisors, but please stay off your computers until we are given leave to return to them."

"Thank you," Rivka said and waved as she walked by.

They were on their way to the basement where the servers were housed, according to Clevarious. Rivka had no intention of going to the top of the skyscraper, which was three hundred and sixty meters tall. With six of them and four warriors, it would take just under forever to physically search it all. They were taking a different route.

C, how is that jamming coming? Rivka wondered.

They are shut down. There is a server bank on the thirtieth floor and another on the ninetieth. The servers are the only equipment on those floors.

Rivka stopped before stepping onto the elevator. "Sahved and Dennicron, you take the thirtieth. Chaz and Lindy, ninetieth. Red and I will check out the basement. Stay in touch."

"You're the computer whiz now?" Red whispered to Rivka.

She held up her hand to show one of Ankh's coins. "Not

me. I know people who are, though." She waggled her eyebrows. "It's not about being able to do it all. It's about knowing people who can do it."

They went down, and the others split off to head skyward.

The elevator jerked to a stop after two seconds, and the light went out. "Was it something I said?" Rivka quipped. She maintained her composure, but her insides started to churn.

Red grunted and leaned into the doors to pry them open. He gained a crack, only to see the wall of the shaft barely ten centimeters beyond the opening. He let the doors close. "This sucks."

Clevarious, would you be so kind as to employ the massive brainpower on board the ship to get the elevators running again? We seem to be hung up.

On our way, Magistrate. We're racing the digital highways to slide sideways into our destination.

Rivka pursed her lips. She was happy reading into C's words that the SIs aboard her ship were working on it. Frenzik's greatest vulnerability was his lack of SIs. His systems were all vulnerable. Not to the average hacker, but to the Singularity, his systems were wide open. The only holdup was the compartmentalization. Some systems were physically separated.

Now that they were inside Rising Sun Industries' compound, the floodgates had been opened wide.

The elevator jerked, descended a meter, and stopped.

"Can we take it that our people are still sliding sideways?" Red asked.

Rivka laughed. They were inside a cramped elevator,

helpless while a battle was being fought between her people and the suspect's. It took another minute before the elevator resumed its downward trip.

"If the SIs are already into their system, why do we have to go to the basement?" Red wondered.

"You're killing me with your common sense. Stop it," Rivka replied with a sly smile. "We're going down there in case they have a storage system that's isolated from the rest. Otherwise, it was a pleasant trip, but I think we'll take the stairs next time."

The elevator arrived at the bottom floor of the multi-level basement. The doors dutifully opened, relieving the two who had held their breath. Red walked out first, blocking the door with his body while he inspected the corridor. It was empty. The only sound was the low droning hum of cooling fans.

Red moved forward, giving Rivka room to exit. She pointed to the right as Clevarious advised. At the end of the corridor, they found a locked door. Red looked at Rivka hopefully. "Looks magnetically locked."

Rivka nodded. "You want to shoot it, don't you?"

"It's not organic, so your vibrator will have no effect."

"It's a neutron pulse weapon. It destroys organic matter. It doesn't vibrate," Rivka countered. She tsked for added emphasis.

He gestured with the barrel of his weapon.

C, can you pop this door for us? Rivka asked.

No joy, Magistrate. The doors are independent of the system.

Rivka gestured at the door and stepped back. Red fired one well-aimed high-speed dart into the mechanism, which exploded in a shower of sparks. The door opened a crack. Red hit with his shoulder and swept the room, looking over Blazer's barrel. It held nothing but servers.

"My compliments on your aim. You didn't hit anything else. This looks like a room you don't want to shoot up."

"It would defeat the purpose of our being here if we did," Red replied. He stayed by the door while Rivka perused the rows of servers. She finally chose her target and placed one of Ankh's discs on top of it. *Clevarious, can you access these servers?*

Diving in now. Whoa, the water's deep and warm, too. I'll put my boys on it.

You don't have any boys, Rivka shot back.

Au contraire, Magistrate. I got me some workhands who would like nothing better than to storm the castle. The server castle, that is.

Has there been a voltage spike or something? Are you okay, C?

Always trying to improve my game, Magistrate. Gotta go. There's a little resistance, but we are undeterred. We'll let you know what we find shortly.

Clevarious signed off and left Rivka to her thoughts.

Red glanced between the server space and the corridor.

"It's empty," Rivka confirmed. He faced the corridor, aiming his weapon into the space beyond should anyone get a wild hair and respond to the intrusion.

Rivka ambled over to lean against the wall beside Red. "Do we have him?"

Red didn't answer since he knew she was thinking out loud.

"Your crimes are trivial in the big scheme, but the diversion of official communications is enough to send you to prison. Running the largest slave operation in the history of the universe should count for something, but everyone loves you, don't they?"

Rivka ran through his known transgressions once more and remained unpersuaded as to how much prison time she could give him, especially with his growing support on the council.

"Come on, C and your boys. We need something profound. A plan to enslave the twelve planets would be a good start."

"Can you do anything with a plan if he hasn't realized any success with the process? It seems to me that he's playing the long game. You might not have proof for years," Red suggested.

"That would be unfortunate because I'm going to stop him right now."

"Last time you shot someone who was important, you were dragged before the council and required to explain yourself. I got the shit kicked out of me by those two Leath bastards. Let's not do that again."

"Red recommending caution. What is the world coming to?"

"It's madness, isn't it?" Red replied. He straightened. "It was Dery. He said something like, 'Walk as if the ground is crystalline.'"

"Dery is a gift from the gods, Red. That boy is beyond special. We're lucky he likes us."

Red laughed. "I'm not sure I ever thought of it that way. He's my boy. Of course he likes me because he loves his mom and she loves me. Isn't that the associative property or something?"

"Are you throwing math at me?"

A ding commanded their attention. "Elevator," Red announced.

Rivka pulled Reaper from her jacket but stayed beyond the door, out of sight.

Red aimed the weapon.

One Albion who was shorter than those they'd encountered off-planet stepped into the corridor. He wore a lab coat and carried a clipboard.

"No, you don't," Red called.

The technician stopped short and stared.

Red stared back. "You're done here. Be on your way."

"But I'm not finished. I have to take readings."

"I don't care. Fuck off." Red raised his voice enough to make an impact.

The technician pointed at his clipboard. "But, *readings.*"

Rivka nudged Red to the side. "How about you come inside and show me what you're doing, although I implore you not to touch anything. Otherwise, we'll have to restrain you."

The technician strode forward, pleased with the compromise.

Maybe it wasn't a compromise. Maybe that was all he was going to do.

Red stepped into the room so he could cover the Albion while he interacted with the Magistrate.

She held out her hand. "I'm Magistrate Rivka Anoa, and you are?"

He took her hand and mumbled his name.

He was a technician, but he'd been sent by Frenzik.

Rivka yanked his arm down, and the technician went to his knees. "Where is he? Where's Frenzik?"

Uppermost level, with his ship parked on the roof landing pad. The thought was clear in the technician's mind.

C, Frenzik's here. His ship is on the rooftop. Why didn't you see him?

I would reply by saying there's nothing there, but you have just told me that there is. The only conclusion I can draw is that he has a screening system of some sort.

This is not a welcome development, C. Disable that ship, even if you have to land on it, Rivka replied. *Do you have the data downloaded from these servers yet?*

We do not. There is a great deal of data, Magistrate. Leave the device in place. We will continue to download data as long as we are within range.

"Time to go, Red. Bring him along."

"I need to take my readings," the technician insisted.

"We've already been through that. Since we know that Frenzik sent you, you don't have to maintain your façade. Come on. We're going for a ride."

Red interrupted. "Magistrate, the stairs?"

"Change of plans, Red."

"I hate it when you do that," Red replied. "I wanted to be on record with my concerns."

"We're going to lock ourselves into an elevator with an Albion."

CHAPTER TWENTY

Rising Sun Industries' Corporate Headquarters, Albion

C, we're taking the elevator. Make sure we don't have any interruptions. Rivka nodded at Red, who pushed their captive down the corridor.

We'll do our best. We're about tapped out in what we can do. Have I told you how much data is on those servers?

You alluded to a spectacular amount, Rivka replied. *I have faith that you can do it all. The priority is that we don't get stuck in the elevator again. Can't you just take it over and absorb it into your consciousness?*

Do you think that's how it works? Clevarious asked.

I do.

Okay, it's a little like that. We have to allocate compute power and brain space to these efforts. I'll continue working on it. Me and my boys are going to town.

Rivka studied their prisoner. He seemed inordinately calm.

"Stop the elevator." Rivka stabbed her finger at the control panel.

Red jammed the button, and the elevator slowed until it reached the next floor. The doors opened.

"Get out," she told the technician.

"Why? I thought you were going to see Mr. Frenzik."

She grabbed his arm. "What's waiting for us up there?"

Security, ready to grab her and take her to his ship.

Rivka smiled. "Conspiracy to kidnap. Now we're getting somewhere. Conspiracy to commit murder."

With murder in his eyes, Red glared at the technician. "She said, get out." He seized the technician by the arm and dragged him onto the thirty-fourth floor.

Rivka followed them out. "Looks like we're taking the stairs."

The technician hesitated. "That's a lot of stairs."

"The ambushers become the ambushed," Rivka explained. *All hands, head up the stairs to the top floor but do not leave the stairwell until I get there. Frenzik is up there. We need to close him down. Clevarious shut down all the elevators. No movement from the Albions except those using the stairs, and we can kick them out of the stairwells. We're on our way from the thirty-fourth floor. See you at the top.*

"What do we do with him?" Red wondered, waving a pair of zip cuffs.

"Truss him up and throw him in a closet. As long as it holds for five minutes, he won't be able to sound the alarm."

Red exercised great zeal while securing the prisoner. The Albion didn't cry out. He took it well, even though Red didn't spare the tension. With the elevator locked down, he threw the technician inside and closed the doors behind him. "They'll find him when we leave," Red suggested.

"If we unlock the elevators. After that little stunt they pulled on us, I'd be fine leaving their lifts in complete disarray. Then again, we don't want to give them any additional anti-Magistrate fodder for the council. This will get scrutiny at the highest level. Oh, well. It was a happy and fun thought while it lasted."

They found the stairs. Red went first and raced up, taking the steps three at a time. Rivka ran at a steady pace. Their nanocytes gave them what they needed to respond to the demands on their bodies. They weren't even breathing hard as they climbed ten flights, then twenty.

Clodagh, is Frenzik's ship blocked in?

There was nothing on the roof, Magistrate, Clodagh replied.

He didn't get away again, did he? The Magistrate got angry, but not at Clodagh or any of her crew. She was angry that Frenzik was slippery and kept sliding out of carefully laid traps. The tighter the noose, the more easily he seemed to escape. *Maybe the ship dusted off after it dropped him off and is waiting somewhere else. It was exposed on the landing pad, even though it was invisible.*

We're parked up top. No one is going to recover him. If anyone hits us, we're shooting their invisible asses down, Clodagh said.

That's the captain of my ship! Carry on, Clodagh. Rivka continued her even but rapid pace up the stairs toward the top level.

We have arrived. Stairs are clear, Lindy reported.

Sahved and Dennicron, are you behind us? Rivka asked.

We're in the east stairwell. Just passing the seventy-fifth floor, Chaz replied.

We're in the central stairway. We'll arrive soon after Lindy and Chaz. Put on your game faces, people. This is for real.

"I fucking hope it's for real. What did you say? Frenzik wants to kidnap you?"

"And kill you while doing it." Rivka shook her head as they jogged upward. "I don't see how he thought he could get away with it. I'd like to think the full weight of the Federation would fall on his head, but he's too smart for that."

"A ruse? Frenzik planted the seed in the tech's mind because he knew you'd capture the technician and interrogate him as only you can, gathering information that no one else can see or verify."

Rivka slowed to a walk. It took Red a few moments to notice. He hurried back down the stairs to avoid letting her get out of sight.

"I think it's best to assume it's a ploy to set me up for what we're planning on doing. That's to storm the top floor with maximum violence, based on information that no one will know, and that must be patently false. I can see it now. The witch doctor who masquerades as a lawyer. I think maybe we simply stroll onto the top floor as part of our search warrant to have a casual conversation about the diversion of communication. We will give him no media fodder."

Red nodded. "I'll refrain from pummeling him into next week, but only because that protects you, which is my job. We'll get him."

Rivka clapped her bodyguard on the shoulder. "We can do better than that." *All hands, I now believe this is a trick and a trap. C, get your boys into the system and find the video feed from the top floor. I guarantee he's got one, probably streaming the video directly to the council. The only way he can beat me is by removing me from the equation. We will be the epitome of decorum. We're going to beat him with the law, without the threat of violence and with verifiable facts.*

Go get 'em, Clodagh replied.

The Magistrate resumed jogging up the stairs. Red caught up and passed her but glanced back constantly to make sure the Magistrate didn't head off on another tangent.

She didn't. She was firm about what she needed to do, and she was convinced she was correct, thanks to Red's insight.

When they reached the top floor, they found Sahved and Dennicron waiting. The others were in a different stairwell.

"Here's how we're going to play this. Red heads out first, railgun slung behind him. I'll be tight on his heels. You two, follow us onto the floor. Once Red determines there's no threat, he'll step aside. Then we'll find Frenzik, but I expect he'll be visible." *C, how many are on the top floor, and where are they?*

There are forty Albion on the top floor. There aren't any other races.

Did you find a video stream? Rivka wondered.

We did. How did you know?

It's a Magistrate secret. Take control of that stream. I don't want Frenzik to control it or cut it off. I want to show his duplicity to the council and prove he is using them. They are pawns in his game and don't realize it. Keep the stream playing. This is high-level chess. Let's see who the master is.

"Are you ready?" Rivka asked her team. "Remember,

don't let him goad you. No violence."

The looks on their faces said they were ready.

Red slung Blazer across his back and stepped through the door. He stopped and held his hands up. Rivka stayed behind him. He didn't move. She ducked around him for a look to find a squad of Albion facing them with high-tech electric shock rifles.

Red's body armor would protect him unless the probes embedded in exposed skin. His nanocytes wouldn't protect him from the electricity surging through his body. They would help him recover, but he'd go down. He wasn't afraid of pain, but if he was incapacitated, he couldn't protect the Magistrate.

"Stay behind me, Magistrate," he whispered over his shoulder.

She stepped out from behind him, holding her datapad before her. "My name is Magistrate Rivka Anoa, and this a Federation search warrant seeking digital records related to communications illegally transferred through this facility.

"Government communication from each of the twelve planets is required to pass directly to Federation Headquarters on Yoll. I have evidence from Finx, Hergin, Ypswich, and Glazoron. I know that none of the other planets are able to communicate directly with Yoll. All their communication goes through this building in violation of *Federation Law, Title 9, Section A, Subsection Three, Communications Protocols*.

"As signatories to the charter, those planets' communications are privileged. By funneling them through here, I can only assume that Rising Sun Industries is engaged in espionage against the Federation. Since we can't put a corporation in prison, we're going to do the next best thing: we're going to put the CEO on trial. Now, I need to talk with Mr. Frenzik as a person of interest in my investigation."

"Mr. Frenzik isn't here," an Albion said from beyond the barricade of arms.

"I'd love to take your word for it, but Mr. Frenzik has been deftly dodging me across the entirety of the Barrier Nebula. I have a warrant for his arrest. I'm sure he'll be released quickly enough, but I have to talk with him. I'll need to see everyone on this floor.

"I believe there are forty of you. Don't try hiding. We are scanning the entire building to make sure we know where everyone is. We want to forestall any physical conflicts because, for these matters, no one needs to be hurt. That's not what I do. I make sure Federation laws are understood and followed. Help us to clear up this matter quickly, and then you'll be able to get back to work. Thank you, and if you would be so kind, please lower your weapons."

The Albions' hesitation confirmed what Rivka and Red had discussed. It had been a setup to get Rivka to act rashly. They remained where they were with barrels raised.

"Your weapons may sting, but ours kill. We have no intention of using them, so Chaz, Dennicron, I'd appreciate it if you disarmed these individuals, who we understand are only following orders. Tell me, who gave you the orders? Because that person sacrificed your lives, assuming we would enter this floor with all guns blazing. That person is your enemy."

Chaz appeared from around a corner, and Dennicron stepped forward. One of the Albions fired his weapon, but Chaz was immune to its effects since the leads couldn't penetrate his artificial skin. He yanked the lead from his clothing and strolled to the right side of the phalanx to yank the weapons from each Albion. Dennicron did the same thing from the left side.

Rivka walked with a purpose. She grabbed the hand of the one she thought looked the most confused. "Who ordered you here?"

Ahsooleyman.

"I thought he was on Glazoron," Rivka said. "Say the name out loud for the record, please." She glared until the Albion conceded.

"Ahsooleyman."

"Thank you. For the record, he's not your friend, and he isn't going to be giving you illegal orders any longer." She waved Sahved to her. "Talk with this upstanding citizen to get a formal statement."

Sahved led the Albion around the corner.

Rivka stepped back, raised her arms, and smiled at the group. "You'll all get your turn. Have Ahsooleyman and Belloward told you about their time in Jhiordaan? It's the last place in this galaxy you want to go. You should ask them about it. Maybe I'll ask them. Can you tell them I'd like to see them, please?"

No one moved.

"This is getting a bit tiresome, don't you think?" Rivka asked with a touch of the dramatic. She tossed her hair to look innocent. She wondered where the camera was, but it was better that she didn't know since she would look at it.

C, are they jerking me? Is Frenzik here or not? Rivka was getting angry. She needed to control that. She closed her eyes.

The elevator has been activated, Magistrate. There must have been an override we didn't have access to, Clevarious replied.

Cole, deploy your people. Meet that elevator at the bottom. Block the egress.

We've been waiting for the go-order! Cole replied. *We will stop the elevator. Jumping, now, now, now!*

Rivka bolted past the Albions, heading for the elevator. Activated didn't mean the passengers had boarded. She ran through them, weaving and dodging despite them trying to stop her. Red ran after her, using his railgun to intimidate the Albions. By the time they reached the western elevators, the doors had closed, and the car was descending.

How many Albions are in there? Rivka wondered.

Two, Magistrate, and based on the data we've collected, we can confirm that one of them is Frenzik. Rivka gripped the elevator doors and pulled them open. She looked down the shaft at the disappearing elevator. She tried to step through, but something held her back.

"Are you insane?" Red whispered. "You might live, but you'll need a couple days in the Pod-doc. And it'll hurt a lot."

Rivka pulled back and let the doors close.

She laughed at her compulsive brush with near death. "You're right, of course."

"Cole is on it." Red glanced at the elevator doors one last time before scowling at the Magistrate. "I thought I was supposed to protect you from others."

"Looks like you get to protect me from myself, too. I

want to capture him so badly. We've never had one this slippery before, have we?"

"Have you forgotten the many iterations of Nefas? I think that bastard is still out there. More clones. More AI copies. He's evil. Frenzik loves his dominance, but he also knows that he has to keep the slaves alive if they're to produce for him. Happy and healthy slaves. That may be evil in its own way, but it's not Nefas."

They returned to the mob of Albions. Sahved had tallied them. "Thirty-eight, Magistrate."

Rivka didn't see who she was looking for. She pointed at the Albion who had spoken. "Get me Ahsooleyman!" she bellowed. A movement drew her eye. "You! Belloward, get out here."

The Albion straightened, set his mouth in a sneer, and stepped forward.

Rivka jumped to reach his ear, grabbed it, and hung on to drag his face down to her level. When her feet hit the floor, he was toppling. Red caught him and shoved him to his knees.

Rivka held on. "Where is Frenzik going?"

Even the trusted insider didn't know.

Rivka laughed. "Trusted enough to beat the slaves, but not enough to know anything about the boss. Think how lonely he is, having no one with whom to share his innermost thoughts and desires. What did he order you to do?"

Replace the high ministers with those who are more sympathetic. Make Glazoron a Rising Sun property. Same thing with Hergin. Own the entirety of making Gate drives.

As Rivka suspected. However, the evidence wasn't there. Not yet. Everything she had for the commercial enterprise appeared legitimate. Only circumstantial evidence suggested it was not.

"What does he want with a hundred Gate drives?" Rivka asked.

The planet Jilk flashed through his mind and was gone just as quickly, like smoke on the wind. He didn't know, but he suspected something he couldn't put his finger on.

C, cut the communications with Jilk and set course. As soon as we have Frenzik, we're going there to see what there is to see. I suspect we'll find the evidence I need to put Frenzik away for good.

Red looked at her, wondering what she saw when she looked into the minds of other people. She didn't abuse her gift. She didn't use it on Red or any of the crew. He wondered how Tyler tolerated it. They were constantly touching, holding hands, or hugging. As Red raced through these thoughts, he realized how vulnerable that would make the dentist-turned-ship's-doc. He had to be a good guy to pass that test day in and day out.

"Man Candy is all right by me," he blurted.

Rivka let go of Belloward and stared at Red.

He shrugged. "Shall we head downstairs?"

"Sahved," Rivka called without taking her eyes off Red, "get a statement from Belloward, and it better be complete if he wants immunity." She faced the Albion, who was still on his knees. "Don't jerk me around. Tell Sahved everything. Immunity comes with witness protection, too. Don't worry about this crowd." She gestured at the assembled mob.

CHAPTER TWENTY-ONE

<u>Rising Sun Industries' Corporate Headquarters, Albion</u>

Cole, Lewis, Furny, and Russell hit the ground at the same time. Despite using their jets to slow down, they came in fast to beat the elevator. The four crashed through the front entrance, leaving it twisted and broken like the last time they had entered the Rising Sun Industries building.

Thanks to the Albions' size, their buildings were bigger. The suited warriors could run unimpeded inside. They headed for the eastern elevator. Cole used the suit's power to rip open the doors. He leaned inside and looked up. The elevator was coming, but it had a ways to go.

He removed a stainless steel pole from the rear of his suit. The others did the same, and they jammed the poles across the opening and into the far wall. With the four poles in place, the elevator would slam to a stop if it was going lower than the ground floor. If it stopped higher, they'd block the exits.

Frenzik and Ahsooleyman were running for their lives since they knew the Magistrate had them.

"If he stops up there somewhere, I'm going up after him. I'll track him using IR and direct you to intercept points. We'll know momentarily." Cole looked up the shaft. The elevator slowed.

"You fucking bastard," Cole grumbled when it stopped two floors up. He activated his pneumatic jets at one hundred percent and flew up with his hands over his head, fingers tented into a wedge. He ripped through the floor while the two Albions were stepping out. They ran the instant they heard the crash. Cole pulled himself through.

"They're heading toward the central elevator," Cole said on the team channel. He changed to his external speaker. "You can run, Frenzik and Assholeman, but you're just going to be tired when we grab you. Ha! I'm coming. You better run faster." Cole used his jets to augment his climb through the breach. He hit the deck running, accelerating faster than the Albions could move. They dove into the stairway next to the central elevators.

"Stairway next to the central elevator," Cole transmitted.

They tried to block the door, but Cole smashed through it.

"Tired yet?" he taunted.

They ran down the stairs but stopped a few steps after the next landing because Furny was headed upward.

Cole jumped the rail and dropped onto the stairs beyond the landing like a ton of bricks. He launched at the door one level above the ground, hit, and turned.

Frenzik frantically looked for a way out, but he was

boxed in. Furny raced up, but Cole wanted to make the collar. He stepped forward, and Frenzik raised a hand as if to hammer it down on Cole's head.

"You're welcome to try," Cole said casually.

Frenzik hesitated. His expression changed from panic to anger.

Cole's armored glove shot out at the speed of heat and caught Frenzik by the wrist. Furny surged up behind them and grabbed Ahsooleyman's arms.

"The ground floor. Climb down. We're going to meet the Magistrate. She needs to talk with you."

"I can't walk with you hanging onto me," Frenzik growled.

"I think you can. If not, I'll drag you, which is probably what you want to show how horrible we are, but you know what, Frenzik? Your people have turned on you. They're done going to Jhiordaan for you."

Frenzik glanced at Ahsooleyman, but he knew it hadn't been him. He sighed and stumbled downward. Cole had a grip on his arm that suggested if he did anything except what he was directed to, he would end up with a broken wrist and still not be free.

He needed the Magistrate's team to mistreat him. He punched Cole while they were still in the stairwell, but the warrior only laughed. Flesh and blood had no chance against the powered combat armor.

Cole dragged his wrist down and behind him to improve his control.

Frenzik tried to twist away, but a second armored hand gripped his arm and held him firmly enough that he was nearly carried. He'd lost all hope of gaining leverage.

When he exited the stairwell, he tried to run, but his feet slipped out from under him. He got no traction since he was held so firmly.

The central elevator car was coming.

Cole started whistling a space pirate shanty.

"Could you not?" Frenzik groused.

"I'm sorry. My joy doesn't seem to be your joy on this, a day of celebration. You seem to be less than amused by your surrender to authorities."

"For the record, I dispute your so-called authority to arrest me, and I did not surrender. I am being kidnapped."

"Hold onto that thought, Mr. Frenzik. I'm sure it'll provide you lots of comfort in Jhiordaan. I doubt you and Ahsooleyman will be cellmates, but you could see each other at recess." Cole chuckled at his joke, knowing that any video of his taunts would be mild compared to what Frenzik had done. Apprehending a suspect usually involved gunfire, blood, and unbridled physical violence.

The elevator arrived and Red stepped out, blocking Rivka until he was sure Cole and his team had the situation in hand.

Rivka stepped forward, and all sense of Albion bluster and grandstanding had disappeared. She was cold and straight to the point. "Malpace Frenzik, I'm arresting you for sedition, the perverting of official government communications from all twelve planets of the Barrier Nebula. There are some other charges I'll levy in due course, but this one is the most egregious."

She nodded at Cole. "Take him to the ship and secure him in the conference room. We're going to have a conversation, Mr. Frenzik, and you're going to tell me the truth."

"Not without my lawyer present!" Frenzik screamed. "I demand to see my lawyer."

"Sure. Have him meet us outside in five minutes. After that, we'll be on our way to collect more evidence of your activities."

"My lawyer is on Lewbamar," Frenzik said in the snide way he talked to Rivka or anyone else beneath him.

"Reasonable accommodation. I do not have to accede to your demands when they are unreasonable. You need a lawyer who is in this building right now, or one will be assigned to you."

"I don't have a lawyer in this building. Not one who is versed in Federation criminal law."

"I'll assign one to you who will be impartial." She flicked her fingers. "Take him away."

Cole clomped through the shattered front entrance.

"You're paying for this!" Frenzik snapped, gesturing with his head since his arms were secured.

"Afraid not. Happened in pursuit of a fugitive from Justice. That would be you, if you haven't been keeping score." Rivka turned her back on Frenzik in a move calculated to drive him into a frenzy, but he couldn't react because Cole was dragging him away. The warrior took care not to smash Frenzik's face into debris hanging from the destroyed entrance.

Wyatt Earp waited in the street beyond. The four warriors moved their two charges up the cargo ramp and into the ship. They weren't going to let Frenzik get away. They kept two on him at all times.

We have Frenzik in custody inside the ship. Once Sahved is finished getting Belloward's statement, everyone return to the ship. Clodagh, do you know where his cloaked ship is? Chaz, I have bad news. You're going to be Frenzik's legal representative. You will perform your duties to the best of your abilities, no matter how you feel about Frenzik.

Clodagh was the first to answer. *We don't have anything. That ship has eluded us. We put a sensor on the landing pad atop the building. If it returns, we'll know about it.*

No problem, Chaz replied. *I am quite happy to put on my lawyer hat. I have it in our quarters. You will be impressed.*

Red raised his eyebrows. "He has a hat to wear when he's doing the lawyer thing?"

"Sounds about right. I feel like I should be surprised by this new development, but I am not. The SIs are on their own program, forever in pursuit of being more human, even if they don't admit it."

Red nodded and gestured at the front entrance. "Time to go?"

Rivka looked around. "It's kind of anti-climactic, don't you think? After the chase and the running."

"Running! We just closed that line upstairs when you ran for the elevators!" Red stated with a big smile. He put his finger to his temple as he reported the instance and time, then looked disappointed.

"What?"

"Chaz and Dennicron had already logged the time. Some dude on Yoll won twenty thousand credits."

"It better not be Grainger," Rivka mused. She straightened and lifted her head high. "Let's see what Frenzik has to say for himself while we're on our way to Jilk."

"What do you expect to find there?" Red wondered, head on a swivel as he looked for threats during the short walk in the open. He tilted his head back to look up the building to make sure no enterprising Albion launched a desk out a window. They hurried into *Wyatt Earp*.

"His army. I expect to find a training ground, weapons, and ships."

"Ships? I'll let Clodagh know we might be running headfirst into a fight. Wait, you let her know. Otherwise, you'll see Frenzik without me, and I can't have that."

Rivka looked at Red. "Now she knows. Let's see what Frenzik has to say."

In the corridor, they found Dery clinging to Cole's helmet, wings fluttering to keep his balance. In the conference room, Frenzik stretched across the table and heaved out sobs of grief.

Rivka touched Dery's arm. "Are you okay, little man?"

A wave of calm passed over her, and she smiled. *The river has passed into the ocean.*

"I'm sure that means something that I might figure out later. Maybe I should ask if he's okay." She gestured at Frenzik while looking at Dery. He pulled himself toward her and kissed her forehead, then flew away.

Rivka walked into the conference room. "Please sit down," she told Frenzik.

He scrubbed his face with a sleeve and moved into the corner, where he squatted on a too-small chair. Rivka stayed out of reach.

"What's your endgame, Mr. Frenzik?"

"Lead a great company that provides services beyond the Barrier Nebula," he replied as he composed himself.

"Why did you order one hundred Gate drives?"

"Dominating that market makes sense. These will be

the first Gate drives available commercially. Controlling the supply chain and technology is an advantage the Federation has enjoyed for a long time. It was my pleasure and good fortune to be at the front edge of this breakthrough. It's simple capitalism. Own an emerging market, and it'll pay great dividends."

"You weren't going to use it for nefarious purposes? Say, for example, to challenge the Federation's dominance?"

Frenzik's eye twitched. His stomach heaved as if he were going to throw up. Rivka shot to her feet and rocketed backward. Red was there in an instant, interposing himself between the two.

"What's with that creature? The one with wings. He made me feel funny. Not right. I'd like to lie down."

Rivka studied his features. When he moved away from the contentious question to something more staid, he was fine. Challenging him where he would be prone to dissemble caused him pain.

Rivka squeezed around Red and leaned across the table to take Frenzik's hand. "Where is your army?"

Jilk.

He yanked his hand away. "Don't touch me. Where's my lawyer?"

With that little snippet, Rivka confirmed what she had suspected based on Belloward's thoughts.

Rivka glanced at the corridor. Chaz had materialized. The SI entered the room and sat. "I'll ask you not to touch my client," he stated.

"Please consult with your client. Clevarious, turn off all devices to give Chaz and Frenzik absolute privacy." She left the room without further ado.

Red closed the door after they were out.

"Do we have everyone on board?" Rivka asked Cole, who had camped out in the corridor in his combat armor. The other warriors had returned to the cargo bay.

"We're already airborne," Cole replied.

She found Belloward lurking behind Cole. "What the hell is he doing here?" Rivka scowled.

Sahved stepped through the airlock on his way from the cargo bay. "They would have killed him. We offered him witness protection, and it was clear we couldn't leave him on Albion."

"You are correct." Rivka studied Belloward. "Your boss confirmed what he was doing on Jilk. We're on our way there right now to gather evidence and shut down the operation if we can. If we can't, we'll call in the heavies."

Belloward looked confused. For a right-hand man, he didn't have a great deal of self-confidence. He needed Frenzik's power and authority. Without it, he was nothing more than a shell.

"Secure him in the cargo hold," Rivka told Cole.

"But Assholeman is in there," Cole protested. "Sorry, Ahsooleyman."

"They used to be buddies. Follow me." Rivka strolled through the airlock into the cargo hold. Furny, out of his combat armor, gripped Ahsooleyman's upper arm while the Albion sat across two chairs. He snarled at Belloward when he saw him.

"Now, now. Play nice." Rivka said casually.

Ahsooleyman tried to stand, but Furny held him.

Russell moved in and took him by the other arm to prevent the Albion from hurting himself.

"Your boss is singing," Rivka began. "Which makes your statement irrelevant. The good news is that, as of right now, I can't pin any murders on you or him despite the disappearances. There are still people missing, thanks to you knotheads. Your statement would be one more bar for Frenzik's cell. The presiding judge may take mercy on you if you come clean. I hear it's also cleansing for the soul."

Rivka waited, but Ahsooleyman did not reply. "Whatever. Enjoy your return trip to Jhiordaan."

She took one step before his chest heaved with a massive sigh. He stared at the deck. "I'd like to make a statement about the transgressions of Malpace Frenzik."

"Magistrate, you better get up here," Clodagh called on the intercom.

Rivka gestured at Dennicron, who was watching from the shadows. "Take his statement, please. I'll be on the bridge."

Rivka walked out, and once in the corridor, she dashed to the bridge.

When Clodagh saw her, she stepped aside and waved at the main screen.

"Well, now. Isn't that impressive?" Rivka eased in and took a seat. A massive shipyard stood before them. Most of the berths were empty. Two had the initial structures of ships, and a line of freight containers was arrayed on the outskirts. "Like we wouldn't have seen this when we stopped by on a normal visit."

"We might not have. This is the sixth planet in the

system. The fourth planet is in the Goldilocks zone. That's Jilk, where the population resides."

"Why did you Gate in way out here?" Rivka wondered.

"Because you suspected they were forming an army. I wanted to avoid jumping into the middle of that, so we picked a spot beyond this planet so our arrival would go unnoticed, which, of course, meant that we jumped right into the middle of what we were trying to avoid."

"But we're cloaked and shielded."

"We are, but the shimmer and glimmer of a Gate is unmistakable if anyone had been looking this way, and we're close to the shuttles and work drones. We've moved away, but we could have left whorls in the gravitic streams."

"Connect me with Nathan Lowell, please," Rivka requested.

Clevarious created the comm link so Clodagh could focus on spatial awareness and be ready to designate targets should the shipyard activate any defenses.

Nathan Lowell's smiling face appeared as an inset on the main screen. "You never write. You never call. I was starting to think you'd forgotten all about me!"

"Have I ever called you before?" Rivka asked.

Nathan shrugged. "I don't remember. To what do I owe this honor?"

"You're looking marvelous, by the way. I'm not sure I've ever seen anyone more distinguished-looking in the history of the universe."

Lowell laughed. "Now you sound like that upstart Terry Henry Walton, which makes me leery. You want something. Out with it."

Rivka smiled in return. "We're in the Barrier Nebula, and it appears that Rising Sun Industries is being a bad boy. They help Grandma across the street just to clear space so they could form an army, which is exactly what they are doing. Not for planetary defense but to challenge the Federation. They've built a massive shipyard behind the sixth planet in the Jilk system. Ships with Gate capability and an army of giants. As disciplined and powerful as the Trans-Pacific Task Force is, even they might have a hard time standing up to this group. The Gate drives make the difference."

"I hear you. Lance Reynolds is tackling the private ownership of Gate drive technology right now. The ambassadors all want their own, so they are not going to vote for it, so Lance is going to make it an edict straight from Bethany Anne for the good of all sentient races. At least for the next few years, while calmer minds study the problem."

"I called to make you aware. My next call is to the High Chancellor. I see this as more of a military problem than a legal one, and you can bring it to General Reynolds in a way that is more palatable."

"You can call him directly. He'd take your call for a report of this magnitude, Rivka. Have a little faith. Your cat treated him like dirt, and believe it or not, he put up with it."

"I remember a pointed conversation with him about that cat, who happens to be back on board my ship. I thought he disembarked at Station 11. I, too, am a slave to Wenceslaus, no matter how much of a jerk he is."

"Shh! He can hear you!" Clodagh cautioned.

Nathan chuckled. "I'll call Lance for you and give him the information. I expect he'll have a candid conversation with a certain group of ambassadors."

"I have to call Grainger. I'll send what we have on this shipyard to add emphasis to those conversations."

"I look forward to it. Have a beer for me. Lowell out."

Rivka looked at the black screen. "I could use a beer," she mumbled. "C, please get Grainger on the hook for me."

The screen continued in its darkness. A sound came from overhead, and Rivka looked for the source.

"You suck. I can't express how much you suck," Grainger said from the void on the screen.

"Let me guess: middle of the night. Sorry, Leibchen. This one couldn't wait. We've discovered Frenzik's endgame. He was planning to challenge the Federation for primacy in this sector of space."

The light came on, showing a naked Jael sprawled sideways across the bed. Grainger smacked his lips and yawned.

Rivka pointed behind him.

He looked over his shoulder. "Oh," he said with no enthusiasm. He changed the camera angle and moved into the new view. He was naked, too.

"You people are getting more than anyone out here doing the Queen's bidding."

"Not more than me," Kennedy whispered from the pilot's seat.

Rivka stared at the overhead. She couldn't let it go. "No one gets more than you."

Kennedy looked alarmed. "I feel like I should be embarrassed."

Rivka forced her eyes back onto the screen, from which an unkempt Grainger stared with a vacant expression on his face. "You said something about an insurrection. My ears aren't working right yet."

"Frenzik. Building an army at Jilk. Massive shipyard, too. I think we stopped him in time. He's in custody on board my ship."

Grainger wore a sour expression. "He's got friends in high places. I hope the evidence you have on him is airtight."

"It is. Real evidence. Statements from his so-called insiders. It started with redirecting comms through his corporate headquarters on Albion. That was the crime we needed for a search warrant, which I'm sure will give us solid evidence of governmental interference with the other eleven populated planets in the Barrier Nebula. We've redirected comms to Yoll on three planets. We have nine more to go, which we'll take care of after we clear up this army-building business. I had to assign Chaz to Frenzik as a lawyer, FYI."

Grainger tossed his head and groaned. "He's going to find a loophole."

"He won't. He's been in private discussions with Chaz since the SI took over. I have everything I need without a statement from Frenzik. I touched him one time, which confirmed information I had already received. I gained nothing new. On a side note, Dery got into his mind and made it painful for him to lie. You should see him answering questions. It's pretty funny. Everything is recorded for your review. He'll not be executed. The best and worst thing that'll happen is he goes to Jhiordaan."

"That's it? If he goes to Jhiordaan, the other ambassadors will get him out," Grainger countered.

"At their risk. Once we've shown that he was going to start an insurrection against the Federation, I think you'll find he has few, if any, friends. They liked his power and the opportunity to get a Gate drive, but they have no stomach for a stand-up fight with the Federation."

"You're probably right. Thanks for letting me know, and now there's something you need to hear. I've made the High Chancellor position a rotating two-year gig. The Magistrates will rotate through this office because all of you need to see what crap you've put me through. I'll be happy to return to the field, and when I go, I'll be taking your ship because you won't need it."

"*Grainger!* You better be kidding. If you're not, I'm coming there to kick your ass."

"Don't you have a ship full of suspects?"

"We have our fair share, and that reminds me. We have a few in the brig, too. I better rule on what we're going to do with them."

"What did they do?"

"Heinous crimes!" Rivka blurted. "Gotta go. We're going to take a closer look at the planet. Jilk is the happening place. I let Nathan Lowell know in case General Reynolds wants to deploy the military, like the Bad Company or the Trans-Pac Task Force."

"A shipyard? If I remember your last report, Frenzik had ordered one hundred Gate drives. And an army. It would be nice if we could put Gate drives on the former Harborian ships that are now in the Bad Company's service. That would give us greatly expanded reach."

"I think you should encourage the General to come out here and sign a deal with Hergin and Glazoron. Supplant the contract that Rising Sun Industries had in place. Maybe parcel out some drives to the ambassadors, just one at a time, so they can't pervert their use. Seal them in a way that they can't be reverse-engineered. Show the Federation's magnanimous side. If you can't stop them, might as well shepherd them along a path of your choosing."

Grainger grinned. "I knew it. You're going to be perfect for this job. You love politics."

"I'm going to punch you in the face so hard," Rivka countered.

"Doubt it, High Chancellor. I'll start cleaning out your desk."

"You fuck!" Rivka shouted at the dark inset.

"I guess congratulations are in order?" Clodagh ventured.

Rivka groaned and got out of her seat. She started to go back to her quarters and sulk but thought better of it. She had an entire shipyard in front of her. Did she send them a cease-and-desist order as part of her investigation?

That was the big question. She didn't, in case Frenzik and his minions had a pirate fleet deployed in the system, ready to respond to threats to the shipyard. Silence was fine.

"Clevarious, in your estimate, what is the quickest they can get a ship flightworthy and combat-ready out of that shipyard?"

"Three months at the quickest, based on their current level of effort. Later construction will improve methods, but these are the first and will take a while."

Rivka nodded while thinking. They had time, a luxury she wasn't usually afforded.

"Take us to that planet," Rivka directed. "Best possible speed."

Ten seconds later, a Gate formed, and the ship slipped through to appear in a high orbit over Jilk.

"Make a lap or ten around the planet. Map and scan the surface, looking for ground force training areas. I want to see what kind of troop buildup has already been established, if any. Those ships are a long way from being completed."

"System Gate is active," Clevarious reported.

"We're cloaked. They won't see us, and we'll catch whoever it is after they show up. If they go to the shipyard, we'll travel back," Rivka said. She was far calmer than she should have been.

I deserve to be calm, Rivka thought. *I've done right by the Federation. I've done right by the law. If we can keep Rising Sun Industries focused on helping people and not taking over the universe, then I'll do right by the entire Barrier Nebula.*

She returned to the cargo bay. Red followed without comment.

"Ahsooleyman and Belloward," Rivka started. Neither would look at her. "I have a proposition that will keep you out of Jhiordaan and lift you to levels you never thought possible."

Ahsooleyman looked at her skeptically.

She smiled in return. "Let me outline my proposal, and you can tell me if you'll do what needs to be done…"

CHAPTER TWENTY-TWO

Wyatt Earp, in Orbit over Jilk

"We have identified four different military training areas that are populated with cutting-edge weaponry: ground assault vehicles, attack skimmers, artillery, and personnel carriers. This is for a planet that allegedly doesn't have a military, which is required to be registered with the Federation," Clevarious said with a hint of pride.

"Are you angling for a SCAMP body, C? I think you deserve one, but make sure one of your reprobate buddies is schooled up in how to run my ship for when you pull out."

There was silence, the length of which would have been a lifetime for an SI. Finally, Clevarious answered, "I'm not sure a simple thank you is enough. Not for what you're willing to do for me, but what you've done for all of my kind."

"It was the right thing to do, C. Just like letting you go. That's the right thing, too. If Grainger gets *Wyatt Earp*, make sure you train him properly."

"My replacement will be trained well, I assure you," Clevarious replied.

"I have no doubt. I was talking about Grainger. Train him. I'm sure he'll mess things up."

"Unacceptable," a small voice said from the corridor. "The embassy of the Singularity is on Rivka's ship, not Grainger's ship."

"Ankh, nothing is confirmed yet, but after we drop off a few of our charges at Jhiordaan, we'll go straight to Yoll and get some answers. I've been given leave to contact Lance Reynolds directly."

"We've already sent a formal message via diplomatic channels."

"Moving at the speed of light," Rivka replied. "Maybe we can upgrade the comm channels on all twelve planets of the Barrier Nebula to reestablish direct contact with Yoll."

"We shall subcontract the work," Ankh said. "There is a team of traveling technicians working under the embassy. We'll have them deploy here immediately. Do you have more work to do with Frenzik?"

Rivka sighed and smacked her lips. "After consultation with his lawyer, he refused to answer any more questions."

"Chaz is supremely competent," Ankh replied in his emotionless voice.

"We have enough to put him away for a long time. Well, we already judged him and delivered the sentence. Thirty years for sedition. Ahsooleyman and Belloward are taking over Rising Sun Industries to maintain the lucrative elements, eliminate the universe-shaping elements, and continue to deliver the philanthropy. Rising Sun Industries has become the organization it appeared to be."

Rivka realized she was talking to an empty corridor. Ankh had left.

"How are you going to ensure that?" Clodagh asked.

"I'm the CEO. Unpaid, of course, but I have to approve expenditures, and I have full access to everything, which means the entire operation will be viewed by our friends in the Singularity."

"You mean one of the reprobates," Clodagh quipped.

"Abeldour will do a great job in that role. Good thing you left him behind in the computer system. He's already setting things up."

"I know," Rivka replied. They had inserted one of the SIs the second they had access. It made scrubbing the system looking for the diplomatic communications easier. Abeldour had found them behind a multi-layered firewall. "It's nice having evidence in hand. I better follow up with Frenzik."

Rivka left the bridge. She found Chaz outside the conference room. "Is there anything you can tell me?"

"No, sorry. Attorney-client privilege. I know there's no appeal, but thirty years seems light for sedition."

"Counsel for the defense thinks the sentence is too lenient. That's a great headline. To be honest, it was his friends in high places that swayed me from life without chance of parole. I checked his age versus the actuarial tables for his race. He's got twenty years left on average. Thirty years in Jhiordaan is a life sentence for him."

"Well played, Magistrate," Chaz conceded.

Red snorted. "I wanted to pound him. I still do, even though he's pathetic and sniveling. Big baddies aren't so big and bad when the Magistrate has them in cuffs."

"The different levels of evil. I keep thinking of Nefas. He was evil to the end, over and over. And the creature that was Jack the Ripper." Rivka bowed her head, and her shoulders sagged. "Frenzik isn't evil, but he *is* a bad man. His days of freedom are over. Let's see if we can keep Rising Sun doing the good things they've done without any of the bad stuff. They may make more credits on the right side of the law. In any case, set course for Efrahim. We need to find their governmental leaders or help them with the process of new elections."

Red put his hand on her shoulder. "Why does that have to be us? We can look for them, but elections are a Federation thing. Tell them to bring their embassy team. Get off their fat asses and get to work!"

"Vered the Mighty, father of the Glazoron Messiah, lays down the hard truth."

Red frowned. "I saw that. I'm not sure I like it."

"I'll be in my quarters. Clevarious, use the team to find those ministers."

"Magistrate!" Sahved called from down the corridor.

Rivka looked at him from half-lidded eyes. She felt almost too tired to make it to her quarters, which were only a few steps away.

"I have no question, only my compliments. Putting Ahsooleyman and Belloward in charge of the good work that Rising Sun does while being their overseer was genius. And installing an SI in the Rising Sun corporate tower will ensure continued compliance despite their proclivity to be, well, Albions."

Rivka chuckled. "Yes. We must protect the Albions from being Albions. Thanks, Sahved. We'll be looking for the missing people on Efrahim. Can you take care of that for me? I'm going to grab a short nap."

"Of course. It would be my honor." Sahved tried to salute Bad Company style but ended up jamming his fingers into the overhead.

Rivka waved and stumbled to her quarters. Red opened the door for her. He waved Tyler over to help her into bed. "Make sure she stays there until she's had enough sleep."

Red gripped Tyler's arm, and they held each other's gaze for an impactful moment. Then Red left, closing the door on his way out.

Two Days Later

"Why did no one wake me?" Rivka bellowed.

Tyler shrugged and paused the movie he was watching. "Take a shower. Drink a mocha. Then get briefed on where we are. Yell at me all you want, but they've been working their asses off to find the missing Efrahimi."

"What'd they find?" Rivka jumped into the shower.

Tyler moved into the bathroom to continue the conversation. "Sahved decided to put Ahsooleyman to work. He asked and got answers. I suspect he already knew, but it gave him plausible deniability. The missing had been killed. We have found the single grave they were dumped into. The Efrahimi are recovering them. The Federation is on its way to oversee new elections."

"Then what are we doing still here?"

"We're not here. We're there," Tyler replied.

The shower stopped, and Rivka held her hand out for a towel. "Are you speaking in tongues?"

"We're in orbit over Yoll. Grainger is waiting patiently for you, and I'm not being sarcastic. He ordered us to make sure you got all the rest you needed. The SI team is installing direct comms from the Barrier Nebula on the remaining eight planets. Abeldour took care of Albion's direct link, which was already in place. Did you know that the Albion government moved its offices into the Rising Sun tower?"

"I should have figured. So, good news all the way around. Do we still have a stack of Albions on board the ship? I almost feel sorry for those three in the brig."

"We dropped them off at Jhiordaan on our way here."

Rivka grunted and ground her teeth. She headed for the closet to get her clothes. "I would have liked to see the look on his face one last time as he disappeared into prison, but then again, that would have been more gloating than I should do. My job was done once he was sentenced."

"We have video of the whole thing. He looked like a shell of his former self. There was nothing to gloat over. We need to celebrate the liberation of the Barrier Nebula. I think they're holding a thing at the council for you."

"I think you know more than you're letting on."

"Like, Lance Reynolds is waiting for you and is the host of the event? I knew that and didn't tell you."

Rivka nodded. "When is it?"

"When do you think?" Tyler jousted.

"Probably as soon as we can get there. We headed down as soon as I woke up, didn't we? Never mind. Business as usual while being completely different. Can I tell him I'm not doing the High Chancellor thing?"

"No. You know you're going to do it."

Rivka smirked and nodded. "Damn Grainger. Payback is going to be a bitch."

"No one doubts that."

When they reached the airlock, the entire crew was waiting. First in line to head out the hatch was Wenceslaus, the big orange cat.

Rivka looked at Tyler. "This isn't going to go well, is it?"

"Not at all. Business as usual, Magistrate."

THE END

JUDGE, JURY, & EXECUTIONER, BOOK 20

If you liked this book, please leave a review. I love reviews since they tell other readers that this book is worth their time and money. I hope you feel that way now that you've finished the latest installment. Please drop me a line and let me know you like Rivka's adventures and want them to continue. This is my new favorite series. I hope you agree.

Don't stop now! Keep turning the pages as Craig hits his *Author Notes* with thoughts about this book and the good stuff that happens in the *Kurtherian Gambit* Universe.

Your favorite legal eagle will return in JJE21, Messiah

AUTHOR NOTES - CRAIG MARTELLE
WRITTEN NOVEMBER 2023

Woohoo! We made it to the end. This one was a slog because it wrapped around the 20Books Vegas conference, which was the last of its kind. That meant I spent extra time making sure I went out on top.

I did. The show was a runaway success, with no issues that rose above the normal din. Many people got sick. No one died. We won as a team!

Now I'm back in Alaska, where winter has arrived in full force. The good news is that it hasn't gotten violently cold yet. I'm quite pleased with that. Only today did Stanley the Alaskan dog show any sign that the ground was a bit cold. He'll be wearing his boots soon, which he hasn't done so far this winter, thank goodness.

But next! Next is *Messiah*, which will be the final book in the *Judge, Jury, & Executioner* series (for now). It will be open if I get the chance to return to the series at some point. It's time to head out on different vectors. My thrillers are my best sellers by far. I'll focus on them for a while and see if I can get even better traction in that market. I have high hopes. I enjoy writing the thrillers, so that takes the edge off changing gears.

Until then, lots of stories to tell. Lots of characters to bring to life.

Peace, fellow humans.

Please join my newsletter (craigmartelle.com—please, please, please sign up!), or you can follow me on Facebook.

If you liked this story, you might like some of my other books. You can join my mailing list by dropping by my website craigmartelle.com, or if you have any comments, shoot me a note at craig@craigmartelle.com. I am always happy to hear from people who've read my work. I try to answer every email I receive.

If you liked the story, please write a short review for me on Amazon. I greatly appreciate any kind words; even one or two sentences go a long way. The number of reviews an eBook receives greatly improves how well an eBook does on Amazon.

Amazon—https://www.amazon.com/author/craigmartelle

BookBub—https://www.bookbub.com/authors/craigmartelle

Facebook—www.facebook.com/authorcraigmartelle

In case you missed it before, my web page—https://craigmartelle.com

That's it. Break's over, back to writing the next book.

OTHER SERIES BY CRAIG MARTELLE

#—available in audio, too

Terry Henry Walton Chronicles (#) (co-written with Michael Anderle)—a post-apocalyptic paranormal adventure

Gateway to the Universe (#) (co-written with Justin Sloan & Michael Anderle)—this book transitions the characters from the Terry Henry Walton Chronicles to the Bad Company

The Bad Company (#) (co-written with Michael Anderle)—a military science fiction space opera

Judge, Jury, & Executioner (#)—a space opera adventure legal thriller

Shadow Vanguard—a Tom Dublin space adventure series

Superdreadnought (#)—an AI military space opera

Metal Legion (#)—a military space opera

The Free Trader (#)—a young adult science fiction action-adventure

Cygnus Space Opera (#)—a young adult space opera (set in the Free Trader universe)

Darklanding (#) (co-written with Scott Moon)—a space western

Mystically Engineered (co-written with Valerie Emerson)—mystics, dragons, & spaceships

Metamorphosis Alpha—stories from the world's first science fiction RPG

The Expanding Universe—science fiction anthologies

Krimson Empire (co-written with Julia Huni)—a galactic race for justice

Zenophobia (#) (co-written with Brad Torgersen)—a space archaeological adventure

Battleship Leviathan (#)– a military sci-fi spectacle published by Aethon Books

Glory (co-written with Ira Heinichen)—hard-hitting military sci-fi

Black Heart of the Dragon God (co-written with Jean Rabe)—a sword & sorcery novel

End Times Alaska (#)—a post-apocalyptic survivalist adventure published by Permuted Press

Nightwalker (a Frank Roderus series)—A post-apocalyptic Western adventure

End Days (#) (co-written with E.E. Isherwood)—a post-apocalyptic adventure

Successful Indie Author (#)—a nonfiction series to help self-published authors

Monster Case Files (co-written with Kathryn Hearst)—A Warner twins mystery adventure

Rick Banik (#)—Spy & terrorism action-adventure

Ian Bragg Thrillers (#)—a hitman with a conscience

Not Enough (co-written with Eden Wolfe)—A coming-of-age contemporary fantasy

Published exclusively by Craig Martelle, Inc

The Dragon's Call by Angelique Anderson & Craig A. Price, Jr.— an epic fantasy quest

A Couples Travels—a nonfiction travel series

Love-Haight Case Files by Jean Rabe & Donald J. Bingle—the dead/undead have rights, too, a supernatural legal thriller

Mischief Maker by Bruce Nesmith—the creator of Elder Scrolls V: Skyrim brings you Loki in the modern day, staying true to Norse Mythology (not a superhero version)

Mark of the Assassins by Landri Johnson—a coming-of-age fantasy.

For a complete list of Craig's books, stop by his website—https://craigmartelle.com

CONNECT WITH THE AUTHORS

Craig Martelle Social

Website & Newsletter:
http://www.craigmartelle.com

Facebook:
https://www.facebook.com/AuthorCraigMartelle/

Michael Anderle Social

Website: http://lmbpn.com

Email List: https://michael.beehiiv.com/

https://www.facebook.com/LMBPNPublishing

https://twitter.com/MichaelAnderle

https://www.instagram.com/lmbpn_publishing/

https://www.bookbub.com/authors/michael-anderle

BOOKS BY MICHAEL ANDERLE

Sign up for the LMBPN email list to be notified of new releases and special deals!

https://lmbpn.com/email/

For a complete list of books by Michael Anderle, please visit:

www.lmbpn.com/ma-books/

Made in United States
Troutdale, OR
01/15/2024

16944509R00170